A MUTUALLY BENEFICIAL SECRET

The Unexpected Series Book Three

HARPER REED

ISBN: 979-8843291181

Cover Credit—JoY Author Designs

Editor: Jamie Holmes

Dedication

For the over-thinkers, like myself, don't be afraid to take the leap.
There just might be a hot British guy waiting on the other side...

Contents

Chapter One

KITTY BEARD

Piper

New Year's resolutions. They're a load of shit. But for the first time since I was in college, I'm making some. Why, you might ask? That's a great question. I recently left behind everything I know in North Carolina, so I could move to Los Angeles, California for a job I've been telling myself I want. Now that I'm here, though...I'm not so sure.

Today is New Year's Eve, and I'm a single, thirty-one-year-old woman now living in one of the largest cities in the world. Yet, instead of going out, I'm standing in the doorway of my home office, looking dejectedly at my computer and thinking I might as well get some work done.

With a heavy sigh, I force myself to pass by my newly set up and organized office and head down the stairs to do another walk around my new condo. I only moved in three days ago, but all of my boxes are unpacked, and I have nothing left to clean or move around.

The stairs take me to the short hallway that leads to my

small kitchen with its cherrywood cabinets and light-tan countertops. The dining area came furnished with a high-top table that has four chairs, which will probably only be filled with people when my best friends Kenzie and Ella come to visit next month.

The living room on my left is cozy with no windows, thanks to being squished between two other condos and the garage in front of it, but there are at least bright abstract paintings hanging on each wall.

I turn back to the dining room and open the sliding glass door to take in the warm night sky. Nothing around here is quiet, and there aren't any stars to see from my porch, thanks to all the light pollution from the big city.

Damn it, I miss North Carolina and I've only been gone a week. As excited as I am about my job as an editor, I've been having major regrets about taking it for the last couple months.

I thought that was mostly because I'd been forced to work from home for so long while my new office was being constructed, but now that I'm here? I'm still not thrilled. It's a deflating fact I'm trying not to focus on, but it's hard when I have nobody to distract me.

My phone rings, and I race back up the stairs to my bedroom to answer it, hoping it's Kenzie and Ella calling to video chat since it's almost midnight over there.

I frown—even though I really have no reason to—when I spot Shannon's name on the screen instead. She's a coworker, and a nice one at that, who had even been waiting to welcome me when I arrived at my new place for the first time.

"Hey," I answer with a huff, surprised the call hadn't gone to voicemail yet.

"Hi, Piper! I'm so glad you answered. Do you have any

plans tonight?" Her voice is hopeful and much too excited for my current mood.

I glance around my room to find an already-made bed, pictures hung perfectly on the wall, and a bathroom that has been scrubbed clean. Twice.

"Not sure yet," I half-lie. She doesn't need to know I'm a loser with no plans other than possibly working on a book I shouldn't be.

She giggles and then pulls the phone away. "Stop. I need to talk to Piper first."

Shannon must be at home with her husband Matt who she's told me so much about. Great, she's going to invite me to something where I'll be a third wheel. I thought things couldn't get worse, but I was wrong.

"Sorry about that," she says. "Matt and I are headed out to a club where a lot of the crew from our floor will be. I thought maybe you'd like to go with us and meet some of the others more officially before your first day."

Oh. Well, that doesn't sound terrible. At least, I don't think so until I eye the flatscreen on my bedroom wall and the comfy mattress with pillows piled up the headboard. I could grab my laptop, get some words down, and watch my favorite cheesy movies until midnight.

Or I could do what I probably should and go out...

God, why does making that choice feel painful? Maybe because I'm ridiculous.

"Can I think about it for a bit and text you later?" I ask.

As lame as I've been feeling about staying in tonight, I'm not overly excited about the idea of meeting a portion of my coworkers on a night where there will be drinking involved.

While I wait for Shannon to respond, my mind has already completely overthought the evening, and I know I should probably say no now instead of disappointing her later. Maybe one day I won't be so uptight.

My head shakes curtly. *Right.*

"Sure, but I hope you'll come with us. I'll text you the info in case you don't decide until the last minute. It's going to be a lot of fun. I promise," she says with an enthusiastic tone.

"Thanks, Shannon. I'll do my best to make it," I say before hanging up.

I throw myself back onto my bed, draping my arm over my eyes and sighing heavily. "What is wrong with me?"

This is not how I'm going to make things better here. I tried to convince myself that keeping Shannon or any other coworkers at arm's length was a good idea, but a part of me —the pieces that my friends often influence—reminds me that I'm never going to thrive in Los Angeles if I fight every new thing I cross paths with just because I'm homesick.

"So pathetic," I mutter before sitting up.

I decide I should eat and have a cup of tea before I make up my mind for sure. A full stomach and something soothing will clear my head. Hopefully.

This time, I tuck my phone into my back pocket and make my way to the kitchen. My eyes linger on my office, and I step inside the doorway once again. This time, I take in the bunk beds I requested in my furniture allowance so that my two best friends would have their own place to sleep. I frown, missing them. Again. Then, I mentally smack myself.

I made a choice to take this job over six months ago. I knew what saying yes meant. I had time to process. I need to stop wallowing.

Fuck, do I.

I force myself down to the kitchen and open the

cabinets. My groceries were delivered earlier today, so I have plenty of choices. I decide on something warm and comforting: grilled cheese and tomato soup.

Soup goes on the stove first before I begin prepping the bread.

"Hey, Samuel. Play Classic Rock," I tell my Echo and grin when the response isn't a robot but one of my favorite actors. It's the little things in life, right?

Joan Jett streams through the speaker, and I get my late dinner going. Once my buttered sandwich is in the pan, I stir the soup before giving my attention to the coffee maker.

I drop a tea bag into a mug and place it under the spout before pressing the button for hot water and going back to flip my grilled cheese.

My mouth is already watering, so I stir the soup again, then take a sip from the spoon. "Damn, I didn't realize how hungry I was."

As soon as my food is done, I practically inhale every crumb and groan once my plate is clear. I close my eyes and rest my elbows on the counter.

Do I really want to go out to the bar with people I don't know?

My phone rings again, and this time I'm sure it's my friends. My smile grows when I see a video chat request pop up from Kenzie.

I hit accept and smile big. "Happy New Year's Eve!"

Ella's face is in the screen more than Kenzie's as she waves frantically. "We miss you."

"I miss both of you, too." I glance at the clock. There's less than ten minutes until midnight for them. "Shouldn't the two of you be with your men? It's almost twelve."

Kenzie grins. "The bar isn't *that* crowded. They'll find us if they know what's best for them."

Ella shakes her head, and her eyes look around, likely for her husband Owen. They soften when I assume she sees him, but then she turns back to the phone. "What are you doing tonight?"

I shrug at the screen, then catch my face in the lower corner. My light-green eyes look pale, and my chestnut hair is flat, falling past my shoulders. The frown on my face deepens and I tilt my head, brushing my fingers over my already-fair skin, hoping it's not actually as pallid as the phone makes me look.

"Uh, Pipe. You okay?" Ella asks when I don't answer her previous question.

I blink several times and focus on their faces instead. Kenzie's fiery red hair and Elle's soft, caring blue eyes. "Yeah, sorry. Just tired from the move. I don't know if I'm doing anything tonight. A coworker invited me out, but I'm not sure I'm ready for that."

Kenzie scoffs. "Ready for what? Having fun? Making new friends? I love you, Piper, and I know we can't possibly understand how you're feeling right now, but what I do know is that no matter how many miles separate us, no matter what new friends you make, or what you do, the three of us, we're sisters for life. Nothing can change that. Don't be afraid to live out there."

I try to object, but she raises a finger to silence me and continues, "This is what you've wanted, and I know it's scary, but it's time to grab life by the balls and live a little. We didn't force you to do enough of that here, and I don't want you becoming a hermit out there. I won't allow it."

Tears burn in my eyes, but I'm also grinning. "I appreciate the words, but maybe I made a mistake. Maybe I should just come back."

Ella is shaking her head, but before she can say anything, Kenzie's rant goes on. "Fuck that nonsense off right now, Piper Lucille Fitz. You're going to do this. Hell, you've already been doing it from home for months now while you waited for the new building to be finished. The only difference now is your address and the fact that you get to work back in the office. Something you've been wanting as well. Remember that? Remember how much you wanted this promotion and what an accomplishment it is? I know you do, and you should be grinning like a badass bitch, because that's what you are."

I'm laughing and crying by the time she's done. My chest aches with mixed emotions, and I want nothing more than to hug both of them. Instead, I swipe at my tears and sit up a little straighter at the table. "Thank you, Kenz. I'm sure I'll stop being a hot mess soon. It's just...a lot right now. I promise I'm going to try harder."

"So, you're going to go out with the coworker who invited you?" Ella asks, her head tilted and eyes full of hope for me.

I nod. "I think I will. I might not make it to midnight, but I'm going to try."

Kenzie runs a hand through her red locks. "Damn right you are. Go curl your hair, clean up your kitty beard, and wear a sexy dress. If you don't make a real effort, then we won't come to visit you."

"First, kitty beard? That's incredible, even for you. Second?" My eyes narrow at her. "You would *not* cancel your trip."

She raises a brow. "Wouldn't I, though?"

I know better than to continue challenging Kenzie. "Fine. I swear to go tonight, and you two better be here next month as planned."

Ella smiles wide. "We will. Happy New Year, Piper. Love you."

I blow her a kiss and return the smile. "Same to both of you. All the love."

Kenzie throws up a peace sign like a nerd, then the video chat ends.

A part of me really hates that Kenzie was right. About everything.

I've been working toward being an editor with our main company Alliteration Publishing for years now. I always knew if I made it that there would be sacrifices. I didn't realize how unprepared I was for them, but this is a new opportunity I need to take.

A new place at work. A new home. A new year. Hell, maybe even a new me.

I've been the reserved, meek friend of our trio for as long as I can remember, but this is my chance to start over. To be whoever I want.

Those resolutions I've never made before but have been thinking about all day begin to surface again.

1. *Be brave and take real risks.*
2. *Figure out who I am without the predictable life I'm used to.*
3. *Finish the book I've secretly been working on and tell Ella and Kenzie.*

That last one makes my chest tighten with equal parts eagerness and dread. It's the only secret I've kept from my friends: my desire to one day write books instead of editing them.

Though, I'm pretty sure I have to accomplish items one and two before I can tackle number three. I need to channel

Kenzie's bravery and Ella's steadfastness and stop hiding behind my fears.

If there was ever a time for me to do this, it's now. I shouldn't waste the opportunity by wallowing inside my house all night and avoiding life.

I send Shannon a quick text confirming that I'll be meeting them there, then I head to my closet, intent to find the perfect dress to wear.

A woman doesn't start over properly without looking her best.

Chapter Two

ARSE TOASTERS

Colin

BLOODY HELL, I DON'T WANT TO DO THIS. MY BOSS is lucky my mum raised me to be a proper man, or I'd have told him to piss off when he "asked" me to attend the New Year's celebration with the other employees.

It's not that I don't like my coworkers, it's more that I'm their boss and hardly know them yet. Going out to a club with them seems highly inappropriate. I've only been working closely with most of them for a few weeks since I spent my first couple of months with Alliteration Publishing shadowing other departments. I don't feel comfortable enough to just "hang out."

According to Steve, my boss, it's a non-issue for me to worry about crossing lines as long as I'm not dating one of them. Drinking and dancing? Apparently, that's perfectly okay.

With a heavy sigh, I pick invisible lint from my black button-up long-sleeve shirt and swipe at the singular wrinkle in my gray slacks.

"I guess I'm as ready as I'll ever be," I say when I turn to face my cat Sir Charles. Yes, I'm a grown man with his own cat, but he was my mum's before she passed last year, and I couldn't abandon him. Not even when I moved from England to Los Angeles over two months ago.

"Don't scratch the sofa while I'm gone or I swear I will get your claws removed," I threaten before leaving my bedroom.

Charlie, as I like to call the gray long-haired fluff ball, meows and follows me toward the kitchen. He jumps up onto the counter, and I swat at him. Instead of running away, he merely snarls at me. Fucking cat.

I run a hand through my dark-blond hair and groan. "I need a cat trainer."

He meows again, then scurries off toward the hallway.

I grab a bottle of water from the fridge, then snag my keys and wallet from the counter. It's already after ten, and I need to leave, but I'm still not keen on the idea.

Even if I'm in a managing role, though, I'm still the new guy and don't want to piss off my boss so soon.

With heavy footsteps, I make my way from the kitchen and into the garage of the house I'm renting from the publishing company. It has three bedrooms and two bathrooms and looks identical to every other house on the street, except they all have varying paint colors over their stucco siding. Boring and predictable. Nothing like my brick masonry home with views of Hyde Park.

I slide onto the black leather seats inside my Lexus sports car—the only splurge purchase I made when I moved here—and put my foot on the brake before pressing the start button.

The engine roars to life, and I turn the seat heaters on.

It might not be freezing outside, but it's still winter, and I rather like my arse toasters.

Before backing out of the garage, I put the name of the club into my GPS and start the directions. I don't think I'll ever go anywhere in this damn city without using maps. Avoiding traffic is key and, somehow, the apps always know where the best routes are. That's a technology I don't care to understand.

The club is just over twenty minutes away, so I turn on some music and focus on driving. When I arrive, the place is packed, but they at least have valet parking, so I use that to avoid spending the next hour finding a space on a holiday.

"Good evening, sir," the young valet says.

"Evening," I reply with a curt nod before getting out of my car.

He hands me a ticket that I slide into my front pocket as I head toward the front entrance. There's a line to get in, but according to Steve, employees who signed up for the celebration should have their names on the list already.

A bald bouncer-looking guy in a tight black shirt nods toward the plethora of waiting people. "Back of the line is that way, man."

I point to the tablet at his side. "I'm on a list."

He sighs and taps on the screen. "Name?"

"Colin Adamson with Alliteration Publishing."

While he scans whatever he's looking at, I get hopeful he's going to tell me I can't get in, but then he taps something and steps aside. "Go on in. Your group should be in the back left corner of the main floor."

"Great," I reply stiffly.

I move around him and, when the door opens, loud thrumming music hits me. I'm a fan of all genres, but not when they're being blasted in my ears.

I give my shoulders a shake and proceed forward. Everything is dark with soft blue lights being the only thing that helps to make sure I don't run into something—or someone—I shouldn't.

Tables are scattered around the outer edges of the club, and there are at least three bars that I can see as I descend the stairs.

Drunk women and men alike bump into me as I continue forward, attempting to find the path of least resistance.

When I finally make it out of the chaos, I see there are at least a couple dozen people talking or dancing in the back corner. Don't the employees have a life outside of work? Why in the world do they want to hang out together when they are off the clock?

Maybe I just haven't been at the company long enough to see why. Sure, I was willing to move to a new country because of the pay and benefits, but maybe there is more I haven't been looking for yet.

"Colin! I'm glad you could make it," Brian, one of my editors who works a few offices down from me, says.

He's wearing a light-pink collared shirt and white trousers with dark sunglasses covering his eyes, even though there's hardly any light in this place.

He hands me a drink, then runs a hand through his shaggy brown hair. "We didn't think you'd show, mate."

I force a smile to my face. Brian is the only one in the office who has tried to use British phrases to connect with me. I haven't decided what I think of it, but so far, he hasn't seemed condescending, so I've merely smiled at his attempts. Little does he know, thanks to all the editing I've done for American authors, a lot of my British-isms have been beaten out of me.

"Of course. I wouldn't miss this," I lie with a grin on my face. It's not their fault I don't understand why I was forced to show up.

I lift the tall glass Brian handed me to my lips, take a large swig of the cold drink, then gag as half of it goes back into the glass. "Bloody hell, what is that?"

Brian laughs and pats my back. "A Bourbon Tea Cocktail. It grows on you."

The back of my hand wipes over my lips. "*That* is not tea, and it's a disgrace to proper tea everywhere to call it such."

He gives my shoulder a squeeze and guides me forward. "Come on. We'll get you something else. I have a table over here with some of the other guys from our floor."

I follow him to a table and see several pitchers and bottles of alcohol in the middle of four other men, most of whom I recognize, thanks to my time spent in the other departments.

Brian gestures to a seat for me before taking his own and begins introducing me, even to those I've already met.

"In case anyone is too drunk to remember... Everyone, this is Colin. He's the new chief editor on staff for our floor. Colin, this is Matt. He's in design, along with James."

The two in question wave, and I return the gesture. "Nice to see you both again."

"Over here is Thad. He works in accounting. And last, we have Mikey. He's also an editor. I think you've met him?" Brian grabs a pitcher of what I assume to be a light beer, based on its pale color, and pours two glasses.

I nod. "I have, but nice to see and meet everyone again outside of work."

Matt laughs, wrinkles forming around his face. "Damn, man. You're a lucky bastard moving here with that accent. I bet the women have been falling at your feet."

I take a drink of my offered beer and shake my head before answering. "I've been so busy with work that I haven't noticed."

Then, I internally groan, realizing I've just admitted to not sleeping with anyone since I moved here. For single men in a big city, those few months are like an eternity.

Matt holds his drink across the table in cheers. "Well, here's to hoping you get lucky tonight."

Everyone else shouts in agreement, and I take a much longer drink of my beer in hopes the conversation will stray from my sex life.

Thankfully, my wish comes true, and I get to laugh alongside them while listening to the guys talk about past gatherings I'm not familiar with. They clearly have no problem throwing each other under the proverbial bus, and when Mikey starts talking about freezing all of Thad's underwear back when they lived together, I find myself wishing I'd met them sooner.

"You lads are insane, but I'm starting to see that's not a bad thing," I say with a chuckle.

Matt tilts his drink toward me with a huge grin on his face. "Hell no, it's not. Stick with us and we'll show you a thing or two about living life to the fullest."

I'm not sure I'm ready for that drastic of a lifestyle change, but I nod anyway and reach to refill my beer.

Brian pushes my hand away from the pitcher. "How are your dance moves?"

I shrug. "Decent. Why?"

He shakes his head and smiles. "Dude, we're at a club with lots of women, most of who are likely single if they're on the dance floor by themselves. That's heaven for a single guy. Just stay away from any of the ones that work with us. Nobody needs that kind of drama in their life."

Dancing wasn't on my agenda. Hell, I thought I would have left already, but since I'm enjoying my time so far, I decide why the hell not.

What could go wrong by dancing?

Chapter Three

KILLING ME SLOWLY

Piper

THANKS TO MY INNER KENZIE, I'VE LET MY inhibitions go and have nearly drunk myself under the table, but I still feel coherent enough to shake my ass on the dance floor. At least, that's what I tell myself I'm doing.

I very well could be making a fool of myself, but there isn't a part of me that cares. Especially now that Shannon and her husband have left, thanks to her getting a migraine. I don't see any of the people around that they introduced me to earlier.

My resolutions have been at the forefront of my mind all night long and, even as I'm dancing, I remind myself that things have to be different for me here. I can't go home before midnight and be the lame woman who starts the New Year alone in her condo. I just can't be that pathetic or even that *me*.

Watching my two best friends move forward with their lives, finding what and who makes them happy, has played a major role in reevaluating my own situation. I've fought accepting that I need to create a new life here in LA without them, but tonight, with my walls down, I finally realize that if I'm going to do what I've worked so hard for then I need to stop wallowing in the past.

That also means I need to stop being so cautious about everything I do or overthinking things like my resolutions list. This is why I'm still throwing my arms around the dance floor and having the time of my life...all by myself.

Sure, there have been people dancing with me, but it's not the same as having a group of friends at my side. Tonight, though, and every day moving forward, *that* no longer matters.

Not if I'm intent on making sure everything I've done to lead to this moment hasn't been for nothing.

My ass bumps into someone, and I don't bother to apologize since it's happened to me dozens of times already, but then a body hits roughly against my side causing me to lose my footing.

With reflexes too slow to react in any way helpful, thanks to all the alcohol I've had, I mentally prepare myself for my face meeting the ground. This is not going to be good.

Though, before that can happen, strong hands wrap around my waist, jerking me forward until my side is pressed firmly against a hard chest.

"Easy there, darlin'. Are you okay?" a deep and very British voice says in my ear.

Holy shit.

I haven't even laid eyes on this man, and he has my core tightening and skin tingling where he's still touching me. A desperate need to throw myself at him overcomes me.

I don't want to turn around. His accent has a sexy lilt to

it, and I'm afraid he won't look as delicious as he sounds. Even more than that, I'm worried he will.

"Can you hear me?" he asks, tugging on my hips until I'm forced to face him. "I'm really sorry about that. I'm not very good at all this."

My ovaries are having a dance party and screaming at me to ask this man to take me right here in the club, uncaring that there are hundreds of people around us.

I can hardly breathe as I take in his dark-blond hair, light-blue—or maybe gray—eyes, clean-shaven face, and kissable lips.

He waves a hand in front of my face. "Did you hit your head?"

I blink finally and shake my head. "No, sorry. I'm fine."

He leans in closer, and the scent of his woodsy aftershave goes right through me. "What?"

Damn this music.

"I'm okay. Thank you for catching me," I say right into his ear this time, doing my best not to inhale too deeply.

He pulls back and smiles widely, then goes back to dancing, but instead of moving on, he stays close while I stand there like an idiot for a few too many seconds just staring at all the sexiness in front of me.

He's wearing gray slacks and a black collared shirt that buttons up the front and has been left untucked, blocking the view Drunk Piper really wants to see.

Shit. I should probably go get some water before I do something I wouldn't normally, like ask a complete stranger to take me home.

Kenzie and Ella would be proud as hell of me if I did, but I just can't. Even if I want to start living more carefree, a one-night stand is too big of a stretch for me. At least right now.

I turn to head toward the bar, but the same man lightly catches my wrist. His mouth moves, but I don't hear the words he says.

He must see the confusion on my face, because he leans in closer. "It's almost midnight."

My breath hitches. Is he insinuating what I think he is?

"And?" I counter with a smile growing on my face.

He chuckles next to my ear and his breath seeps into my skin, branding me like a hot iron. "And you should stay here. With me."

His accent is killing me slowly. I can't tell him no. The desire to taste his lips on mine is too strong, even though I don't even know his name.

I finally nod, and he grabs my hand, pulling me closer. His hands hold my hips, and I watch as he attempts to find a rhythm to the music. *Attempts* being the operative word.

No wonder this sexy man is still on his own. He can't dance to save his life. Though, his moves are so bad that they're almost endearing.

I try to match his awkwardness and laugh my ass off when I decide I'm worse than he is at this whole thing.

My hands gather my long brunette strands, and I lift them off my neck before turning around. My ass presses against him, giddily feeling something long and hard within his pants as the sexy stranger slows our movements until we finally match paces.

His arm moves, and he pushes the rest of my hair to one shoulder, then presses his lips to my neck.

Shivers race down my back, and everything inside me tightens in anticipation of what might happen next.

The song ends, but he doesn't let go of me and I don't dare make a move to leave. A DJ taps the microphone and starts speaking.

"How are we doing tonight, LA?" he shouts. Cheers echo through the room. "Are we ready for the final countdown to midnight?"

I don't hear any other sound in the room except for the handsome man's voice from behind me. "Absolutely."

People start chanting around us. I assume they're counting down, but I can't be sure as I turn around and meet the stranger's heady gaze.

One of his hands raises and cups my cheek. "I'm going to kiss you unless you have any objections."

"Hell, no, I don't."

He laughs, and I realize the words were said out loud instead of the thought I intended them to be.

Screw it. This is the new Piper. The one who is living her life to the fullest and who is going to do whatever it takes to make sure moving here becomes one of the best choices I've ever made.

My fingers grip his shirt, and I jerk him closer. Shouts sound off all around us, but I don't tear my gaze away from his as I lean closer.

Our lips connect in the next second, and a burst of pleasure shivers its way down my spine while I arch closer to him. His tongue presses forward, and I open for him without hesitation while his hands hold me tightly to his chest.

A faint taste of beer hits my tongue as he devours my mouth with possibly the best kiss I've ever had. I moan against his lips, my toes curl inside my black heels, and I hope I'm giving back as good as I'm getting in my inebriated state.

One of his hands moves over my ass, gripping the bottom of my dress so tightly that I'm pretty sure my cheeks are showing, but I can't find the will to give a damn as my core tightens and screams for me to go home with the delicious slice of man.

Except I know me. Even if I don't always like my reserved nature, I can't let my hormones make this decision. Thankfully, I don't have to.

Mr. British pulls back, holds me by the hips, and grins, showing off dimples I hadn't noticed before. "Care to keep dancing?"

I nod. "That sounds perfect to me."

Everything about this moment feels right, at least for the night, and for the first time since I parked my car in front of my condo, I finally feel like moving here might not be as daunting as I'd been telling myself.

Chapter Four

ELUDE ME

Colin

WAKING UP THE NEXT MORNING IS PAINFUL. NOT because I'm hungover, but because I'm not as young as I used to be. My body is reminding me that thirty-seven isn't anywhere near twenty-one in terms of staying out later than normal and dancing for hours on end.

As I get out of bed, I'm eternally grateful to have today off to recover from the night before. Though, I don't stay in bed. I head toward the shower in hopes I can wash away some of the aches and pains rising inside me.

While I wait for the water to warm up, I recount the previous evening and grin.

That woman.

I don't know who she is, and I stupidly didn't get her name or number before she disappeared around one o'clock. It disappointed me more than I expected it to when I realized she didn't say goodbye. So much so that I have a feeling I'll be back at the same club next week just to see if I might find her again.

And when I do? I won't let much time go by before asking for her information. At least, that will be the plan if I manage to see her again and she doesn't run away.

She was the only one who hadn't been afraid of my terrible dancing. And when I kissed her? My dick had never stood at attention quicker. But I haven't lost hope yet.

By the time I get the beautiful brunette out of my thoughts, I'm done washing up and head for the kitchen before bothering to dress.

Even more than needing to be clean, I require coffee and medication to kick the lingering headache I can feel growing in the back of my head.

Tomorrow will be a better day once I'm back at work. Hell, maybe one of the guys I was hanging out with will even remember my dance partner and, better yet, know her name.

———

UPON ARRIVING TO WORK THE NEXT MORNING, I'M quickly reminded about the staff meeting we're having to welcome all of the new employees that have been starting at the office over the last couple weeks.

Hopefully it won't last long. Since we were closed yesterday for the holiday and I was too tired to get anything done at home, I'm further behind on my work than I'd like to be.

Begrudgingly, I lock my computer and head for the main meeting room. When I arrive, there's a welcome banner strung on the wall with balloons floating at each end. A bit over the top, but then again, that's Steve.

Brian waves when he spots me from across the room,

and I head toward him, sidestepping other employees who seem too chipper for this early in the morning.

"How did you feel after our night out? Hopefully as bad as I did," he says with a spark of evil in his hazel eyes.

"Can't say that I did." I chuckle. "I only had the one beer at the table before we went out on the dance floor."

He groans and lets out a heavy sigh. "Dude. You shouldn't have let me keep going back for more."

"Life is all about learning lessons the hard way," I joke.

Thad and Mikey come over and sit next to us while the room begins to fill as plenty of others walk in. My phone pings with an email from one of our distributors and holds my attention until I hear Steve's voice raise over the room.

"Welcome, everyone, to our first meeting of the year. I'm so glad we can finally all be together now that the construction on our floor has been completed and the holidays are past us. A big thank you to those of you who worked remotely and had patience during a few of our setbacks. I also know it's the day after a long weekend, so I'll get right into the introductions I wanted to make this morning. We have a lot of new faces on the fourth floor, and I want to make sure that we remain as we've always been: a family."

Steve grins as he pauses, his wrinkles deepening the longer he smiles, scanning the room. "When this company was started over fifty years ago, my great-grandfather had big dreams for what we might be able to accomplish, and I'm pleased to know we've not only met them, but we've surpassed what he'd envisioned, something that I give credit to each of you for. Without your individual roles doing their part, this company wouldn't thrive as it does now. I truly believe that."

People begin to clap, and I follow suit. I've heard this

speech before. While I can feel Steve's sincerity in his words and gestures, he preaches it a little too much for my liking. I prefer to put my head down and get work done like I'd been doing the last couple months since joining the company.

"Now, as much as I wish we could sit here all day and chat, I know at least a few of you are eager to get back to work." Steve's eyes land on me for a brief second. "Let me introduce all of our new employees and what their roles are. Some of you may have interacted by phone and email already, but it's always nice to put a face with the name, right?"

A few laughs ring out amongst the crowd as Steve begins asking people to stand up, like we're in a classroom.

Employees from accounting, marketing, distribution, and other departments I didn't get to sit with are called out, and then he even says my name.

"Colin Adamson, please stand for everyone," Steve says with a glint in his eyes. "Colin has been here for a couple months now, but he arrived just after our last quarterly meeting, and given he's one of our lead editors who stays oh-so-busy in his office, I thought putting him in the spotlight would be fun. Don't you all agree?"

I might know deep down that Steve means well, but I really want to kill him right now.

"Come on now, Colin. Stand up." He gestures toward me with one hand. "Don't be shy."

Fucking hell. I rise from my seat and ignore the jests coming from Brian next to me and even the loud gasp followed by murmurs I don't quite catch from someone else in the room.

I wave awkwardly but don't really glance around, in hopes that this moment will be over quickly.

"Colin came to us from a publishing house in London,

and we're so grateful to add his ten years of experience to our company. He's not much of a talker, but because I'm his boss and he can't yell at me, I encourage all of you to go meet him more formally whenever you get the chance if you haven't already."

Steve grins widely at me, and I slink back into my seat, my like of him lessening by the second.

He continues talking and introducing more people, but I don't hear the rest of the names as I work to shake off the unexpected attention.

Brian pokes at my ribs. "Hey, man. Meeting's about over. Be ready to dart toward the door first if you want to avoid talking to people after that introduction."

I glance up and am already feeling better. Normally, I'm not that uncomfortable with large groups, but apparently, today I am. Steve is talking about the newest editor, one I haven't met. At least, I didn't think I had until I turn to look at her.

Piper Fitz.

I'd seen her name on emails and papers and heard others mention her, but given all the remote employees reported to Helen, I'd yet to speak with her myself.

Well, not until two nights ago.

At least, I'm rather positive this Piper is the same woman from the club with her long, flowing chestnut hair, slim waist, and creamy skin.

Half of her face is being shielded by her long strands, and she isn't looking my way, but I'm certain my instincts are accurate.

Damn it. How could my luck be so bad? The first woman to interest me since leaving London, and she's a coworker who is off-limits.

Go fucking figure.

She must have seen me, which is why she's hiding now. Hell, she might have even been the person to gasp when I stood earlier. If so, that tells me she clearly remembers me from New Year's Eve. At least, I hope so.

I wonder if she knows about the lovely clause in our employment contracts about intraoffice romances. Probably. I don't see why else she'd be ignoring me when we both seemed to enjoy our time together the other night.

Thad leans forward and taps my and Brian's knees. "It's a damn shame she works here. But then again, a fling could be fun, too."

Something dark and possessive unfurls in my chest, forcing me to take a deep breath. There is something seriously wrong with me. I didn't even know her name until a minute ago. Well, I didn't know I knew it anyway. I can't be *that* attracted to her already.

A few minutes later, Steve ends the meeting with more of his pep talk words, and I quickly head to the door. I want to watch which direction Piper goes, so that I can attempt to speak with her later when there aren't so many other people around.

She's sticking close to Shannon, who is another editor, one that I've talked with a few times and emailed plenty. Shannon seems to be friends with everyone, so it's no surprise she's taken someone new to the building under her wing.

Previously, I was perfectly okay that the remote employees all reported to another manager, but now? Now, I wish I'd known who Piper was before going to that club.

I observe her closer, taking in her square-framed glasses that she hadn't been wearing the other night. I'm not a fan of them, only because they hide the depth of her green eyes that I remember getting lost in while we were dancing and kissing and touching...

Her long dark hair falls nearly straight around her shoulders and stops at her mid-back. She's wearing black slacks and a light-pink blouse with three small white buttons at the top. Only one is undone, and I'm very eager to undo the others.

Her gaze flicks toward me, and I don't miss the rapid intake of breath she takes before quickly turning in my opposite direction.

I grin and rock on my heels with my hands in my pockets. She did see me, and she certainly remembers me.

Good.

I might prefer to put my head down and avoid everyone else while I work, but this woman... She's not going to be forgotten, and I sure as hell don't intend on letting her elude me.

No, I'm too damn curious now to pretend nothing happened on New Year's Eve with her. Especially with her reaction to seeing me.

Even if I signed an HR policy stating I wouldn't date anyone within the office.

Chapter Five

TANTRIC TONGUE

Piper

THIS ISN'T HAPPENING. NOPE. I REFUSE TO believe that the man I made out with on New Year's is also my new boss. No. Just so many freaking no's.

Shannon has stayed by my side, even though I'm fully aware she didn't buy the "I choked on air and I'm an idiot" excuse I told her when I gasped and then could barely breathe during the meeting.

When Colin stood up, I couldn't believe my eyes. I didn't think I'd ever see him again. I'd ditched him, thanks to my alcohol finally catching up to me and making me unexpectedly sick, a fact that disappointed me to some degree until just five minutes ago, but that isn't the point. The point is that I mouth-fucked my boss, and I haven't the slightest clue how I'm going to handle the situation I seem to have dug myself into.

"Seriously. Now that we're alone, what's going on with you? First-day-in-the-office jitters? Too much coffee? Not enough?" Shannon asks me after we exit the room and stop further down the hallway.

I glance over at her and try to force a smile to my face. When that doesn't work, I distract myself with anything other than Colin's face flashing through my mind.

I take in Shannon's black-and-white blouse and her charcoal pencil skirt along with her maroon Jimmy Choo's I might possibly kill to have. Then, I let my gaze travel back up to meet her concerned face. Deep, ocean-blue eyes are still staring at me, and a strip of her light-blonde hair hangs loosely outside the tight bun the rest of her strands are locked into.

The need to tell someone about Colin is strong, but I read the paperwork when I took this job. I read every tiny little word, and I specifically remember that there are no intra-department relationships allowed.

The last thing I need is for a new coworker to figure out what happened and get me in trouble. I hope Shannon wouldn't stoop that low, but I have to be smart. I don't know her well, and telling her is a risk I'm not willing to take.

Working for Alliteration Publishing has been a dream of mine since I was hired at Bookish Pub as an assistant. I can't give up everything I've worked so hard for, especially not for some guy I randomly kissed on a dance floor. No matter how sexy he looks and delicious he tasted.

Shannon gives my arm a slight shake. "Hey. Seriously. Are you okay?"

I finally nod and smile. Or at least, I hope that's what my face is doing. "Yeah, sorry. Being in the spotlight was a bit much for me. I didn't expect that since I've technically worked for this company for over three years. Plus, I'm not used to being around this many people after working from home for so long."

Shannon throws her arm around me and leads us back to our office area. "Don't worry about a thing. Nobody really pays attention in there anyway, and there were more new people today than normal, so I'm sure nobody saw you trembling in your seat or heard you choke on air. You're totally cool still."

She laughs as I lightly shove her away with a real grin on my face. "Gee, thanks. I didn't think I was *that* bad." Okay, maybe I did, but she didn't need to know that. Or maybe she already did.

"Um. Yes, you were. I only didn't say anything before because *that* would have drawn attention, but let's not talk about the meeting anymore. Have you started Spiro's new book?" she asks, glancing behind me at my desk now that we've arrived at my office door.

I nod and sigh. "Roman is...*everything*." The best part of my job is that I get to pick the genres to edit in and I signed up for all things romance. Sometimes that includes crazy scenarios I don't expect, but most of the time, I get to live vicariously through the fictional heroines. My love life has been rather lackluster, especially once I knew I was moving.

I try to recall the last time I went on a date with a guy more than once, but hell if I can remember. Dread consumes me. Oh, my God. When is the last time I had sex?

The fact that I don't know the exact answer to that question is downright embarrassing.

Shannon laughs. "Damn, Piper. You really get into your work."

My face is flushed, but I let her think it's because I'm

turned on by a fictional character and not because my abstinence has lasted way too fucking long.

"Hey, we can't all be lucky enough to marry the perfect man so young," I tease, trying to get the conversation off me.

She blushes. "I really am a lucky bitch. Alright. Enough talk. I have way too much stuff to get caught up on, and I'm sure you do as well after taking time off for the move. Want to do lunch at one today?"

The fact that Shannon is treating me as if I've been working in the office for months rather than hours warms a piece of my heart I thought went cold when I hugged Ella and Kenzie goodbye back in Charlotte.

"Yeah, that would be great," I say with a smile as I lean against my doorframe.

"And my treat to celebrate your first working day in LA!" She waves and heads two offices down to her desk.

With a wave of my own, I take a few steps forward and close the door behind me. When I get to my chair, I lean back against the charcoal leather material and close my eyes.

I still can't believe *he* works here.

Even worse, that he's the boss I'll now be reporting to directly. Like, how is this my life right now?

Thank God for Shannon. Though, her insistence that I go to that damn club is the reason I'm in this situation. Yes, I realize it isn't really her fault, but as I pick up the manuscript I've been doing first-round edits on between moving and unpacking, I selfishly admit it's easier to lay blame where it doesn't belong than dwell on how the hell I'm going to avoid Colin for as long as possible.

———

I'M FINALLY AT HOME AND HAVE ALREADY changed into my pajamas before pouring myself a glass of white wine. My first day in the office is done, and I managed to do just as I hoped. I didn't see Colin after the morning meeting, but I did see an email from him. One that will require me to be around him tomorrow that he sent right as everyone was leaving for the day.

It was short and to the point, but for some insane reason, I'm still thinking about *why* he called for a meeting and how many people he invited. Holy shit, what if it's just me and he only made it sound like it was going to be a group thing?

He wouldn't do that, would he?

Even worse, what if he doesn't remember me? Could I really be the only one losing my mind right now? When we'd been dancing, he hadn't seemed drunk, but I sure as hell was, so maybe my memory isn't recalling things clearly.

My hands cover my face, and I let out a loud groan. "What the hell am I going to do?"

Call Ella and Kenzie, I think. That's something I should have done as soon as I got in my car, but a part of me doesn't want to make the kiss with Colin into a big deal.

I can't date him, so why do I even need to think about what I'm going to do when I know there isn't anything I *can* do?

Because his tongue made your toes curl, and you have dust bunnies threatening to make a home in your unused vagina.

Okay, that's a very valid reason my subconscious has kindly reminded me of, but it doesn't change the fact that I literally can't date Colin without breaking a clause in my contract at work.

I grab my phone and hit the video button on our group

chat, crossing my fingers that Kenzie and Ella aren't too busy tonight.

Just when I think neither of them are going to answer, Kenzie's mussed auburn hair appears on the screen. "Hey, Pipe. I wasn't sure we'd hear from you tonight."

Her hazel eyes crinkle at the sides as she grins at me.

"Were you about to head to sleep?" I ask when I realize she's leaning against the pillows in bed. Shit, I hadn't thought about how the time difference between California and North Carolina would affect my ability to chat with my best friends.

Kenzie grins, and I hear her boyfriend Bentley mutter, "Don't you fucking dare."

"Bentley was just dosing me with my daily required orgasm. I'm wide awake now."

Ella chooses that moment to join us, and we're both shaking our heads at Kenzie's crass ways.

"He's going to cut you off if you keep talking about your sex life with other people in front of him, including Owen," Ella says, and I can see she's wrapped in a blanket on her couch.

"Were you sleeping?" I ask, trying to ignore the guilt I feel at having called so late. I mean, it's only ten their time, but still. They both have to work tomorrow as well.

Ella grins. "No, I was reading that book you left for me, but Owen is already out, so I snuck out here to call you back without disturbing him."

"At least someone is considerate," Bentley says, then I hear a door slam closed.

Kenzie's Cheshire grin grows bigger as she burrows further into the pillows. "Are you finally going to tell us how your day really was, Pipe? Your short texts were bullshit, by the way, but I'm trying this new thing where

I'm being more considerate of people's need for privacy. Though, I'm only successful about half the time, as you just saw."

A laugh bubbles up inside me. "Well, I appreciate your patience while I processed things."

Ella raises a brow and holds the phone closer. "So, something *did* happen?"

I nod. "Well, kind of. The guy from the club?"

"The one with the tantric tongue?" Kenzie cuts in, waggling her brows.

"That's one way to describe him, but yes. Him. Well, I saw him today," I say with trepidation in my voice.

"Where?" Ella asks.

I bite my lip before answering. If I say what I'm about to out loud, this whole situation is going to become a whole lot more real, and I don't know if I'm ready for that. I realize I've only made out with Colin, but damn it if the kiss hadn't been the best I've ever had.

"At work. He's my new boss. The chief editor I'm supposed to be reporting to now that I'm in the office."

The knot in my stomach builds into a boulder, and I wait anxiously for one of them to say anything to make me feel better, but for the first time ever, neither has anything to say for too many seconds.

Kenzie's face turns serious before she breaks the silence first. "You like him."

I shrug. "I *like* how I felt on that dance floor. I don't even know *him*."

"But you want to," she quickly counters, and I barely manage a nod. "Then, what's the problem? Was he a dick when he saw you today? I'll fly there and kick his ass if so. Nobody insults my Piper."

My heart warms at her threat.

"I'm tempted to lie just so I can see you in person," I lightly joke.

Ella frowns and adjusts her blanket around her shoulders. "We miss you, too. Like crazy."

Kenzie rolls her eyes. "Enough mushy. What happened with club guy, now known as sexy-boss guy? Unless he has a name you'd prefer I use. Though, no promises I will."

I sigh and begin recounting how everything went down earlier and how I hid in my office for the rest of the day, besides when I left for lunch with Shannon, then ending with the email I received about the meeting.

Kenzie lets out a low whistle. "First off, kudos on finding an English guy. I bet his accent alone melted your panties, didn't it? Never mind. Don't answer that. Yet. As far as him being your boss and the intra-department dating rules, can't you just switch departments if you two actually end up dating long term?"

I frown and shake my head. "Our floor is the only one with romance editors. If I moved, then I wouldn't get to do what I came out here for, and I can't accept that."

"Neither would I, so I'm glad you think that way," Ella says. "As far as having to see him in the office, I'd pretend nothing happened, honestly. If there's nothing that can transpire between the two of you, then just move on. That seems to be your only option that you can live with."

She's not wrong, but given I can still remember the feel of Colin's body pressed against mine, I have a really hard time accepting that's the option I should go with.

Kenzie holds up a finger. "Or..." She grins widely. "You could toe the line with him. See what happens, and then maybe *he'd* be willing to switch departments. Men do crazy things for women, and you, Piper Lucille, are priceless. If this guy is smart, he'll see that, and things just might work out."

Shit.

What if Kenzie could be on to something? The fact that I hope so scares the hell out of me, and now I'm even more confused than I was before calling them.

Chapter Six

FORBIDDEN ROMANCE

Colin

WHAT HAVE I DONE? THAT'S A QUESTION I'VE been asking myself ever since I sent the email out before leaving work yesterday.

I have no real reason to meet with the other editors. My only plan as of now is to pull a Steve and have it be more of an editors-only meeting where I tell them a bunch of stuff they should already know.

Though, there is the latest batch of submissions we've received from agents. Normally, I only go over those with the editors they'll be assigned to, but I could use those to fill up some of the time.

Steven appears in my doorway, knocking on the metal frame about ten minutes before I'm due to head to the small conference room I reserved.

I glance up and smile, no longer annoyed with him for putting me in the spotlight yesterday. "Good morning."

"It is a good morning, isn't it? I wanted to stop by and see if there is any way that you can work with the other editors on getting through more of these queries. I received an email from Jameson that he's concerned with our response times and wants to make sure we're not missing out on content that could be good for the company."

Well, isn't this the best news I've ever heard.

"Absolutely. I'm already meeting with the group this morning. Tell Jameson we've had some bumps with the transition into the new building, but I'm certain things will move a lot faster now that we have everyone here working together."

At least I now have real content to go over with everyone instead of floundering like an idiot who only wants—no, needs—to see how the woman he made out with will react to his nearness.

Yeah, I'm acting like a teenager, but I don't care. I'm too damned curious about Piper, given how she ignored me yesterday and kept her door shut all day.

Steve lingers and steps inside my office. "I know you're good at what you do, so don't take this the wrong way. We really are glad to have you here, but if I can suggest an idea to you..."

I smile even though dread quickly fills me. "Of course."

He nods and takes a seat in the chair across from my desk. "What if you teamed up with each of the editors? I know you prefer emails to one-on-one time that takes away from work, but you have a lot of experience, and not everyone on your team does. You could coach them and build trust between the group individually, then all together by having weekly recap meetings of things you've learned until things are moving along a little smoother."

Normally, I'd be annoyed with someone butting in on how I run the staff I'm in charge of, but Steve has just given me everything I need to remain levelheaded about my unique situation with Piper.

"You know, that sounds brilliant. Thanks for the suggestion," I say sincerely, and his face lights up.

"Really?" he asks, voice filled with a bit of shock. "I knew we were going to make a great team. I'm glad to see I was right."

Steve gets more interesting as a boss every time we chat. He almost seems unsure of himself at times like now, but when he's talking about projects, there's no denying how passionate he is for what we do and how much knowledge he has to share.

I just have to remind him of one little thing.

"As long as you don't put the attention on me like you did in the meeting yesterday, then I agree," I say with a slight laugh, even though I'm not joking at all. I don't want to come off as an arsehole.

Steve gets up and lightly slaps the top of my metal desk as he chuckles. "We'll see about that."

Maybe I shouldn't have played that off so coolly.

He leaves before I can say anything else, which is good, because I only have a few minutes to get my act together for the meeting I don't really have planned out yet.

I quickly jot down some of the things that Steve mentioned, then add a few of my own that come to me as my mind starts churning with ideas that will help our team immensely. At least, that's what I hope.

When I arrive to the conference room right on time, I'm impressed to see all six editors there with notepads, talking quietly amongst themselves. Three of the six present —including Piper, who has seemingly found the pen in her hand very interesting—hadn't worked in the building until the last week or so.

Steve had offered to let people stay where they were for Christmas, even though the building has been done for over a month now. At the time, I'd thought it was kind of him. Piper was the last of them to arrive, which now makes me wonder what and who she might have left behind from wherever she came from.

I take my seat and set my papers down on the table in front of me. "Thank you all for joining me on such short notice. I hope not to take too much of your time, but I spoke with Steve about some things and would like to go over them now that we're all together."

Nobody says anything as I meet the eyes of each person in the room, beginning with Brian on my left, followed by Michelle, Kasey, Mikey, Shannon, and then Piper, who is finally looking up.

I smile when our gazes connect, and her green eyes widen before blinking several times. It's not my intention to make her uncomfortable, so I continue.

"With the holidays, settling into the new office, and adjusting to a new team, it's clear our timelines for moving through submissions have slowed down considerably. I've told Steve we'll have no problem increasing the amount of queries we get through each week, and I'm hoping we can all settle on a number to strive for."

Mikey jots a few words down, then looks up at me. "We need to be reading less in order to get through more books."

My head cocks to the side. "Explain."

"Alliteration has always strived to be different from other publishing houses by making what we do more personalized than some of the other bigger companies, but certain things are going to be hurting us, like not getting to certain books quick enough. Agents aren't just sending manuscripts to us when we receive them. They're shopping them several places, and unless we start only reading the first few chapters like most places, then we're never going to get caught up."

He has a point, and it was something I'd mentioned to Steve when I first came on. He said that the editors at least skim all the way through the books before making a decision. His reasoning was that some authors need to shake off their nerves with those first few chapters or they simply overthink them. If we never get past what might be the worst part of the book but is also fixable, how will we know if we've passed on the next bestseller?

I hadn't been able to argue with him then, but now it seems we need to find a compromise.

"How about we settle for this, and I'll let Steve know this is the plan myself? We only read the first five chapters moving forward. No more skimming the remaining chapters. Books that have potential, you can make the choice to read another five chapters or the whole thing. I trust you to make the right call on that. This should allow us to move through them rather fast, yes?"

Several nods of approval go around the room.

"How much of our day do you want spent on editing books we have contracts with and then reading new submissions?" Shannon asks, clicking the end of her pen several times as she speaks.

I make a note about the first five chapters I need to tell Steve about before answering Shannon. "I think we need to decide on our goal of how many submissions we want to get through each day or week before we finalize the balance. If each of you will think about your schedules and give me a number based on only reading five chapters, then we can discuss that in further detail later this week or early next week."

She nods and smiles, seemingly satisfied with my response.

"We're the biggest team on this floor, and I want us to find a workflow that makes everyone's jobs easier. With that being said, we can't figure that out until I've seen what everyone does exactly. I know your roles, but I also know that we each get to the end result a little differently. Steve mentioned it might be a good idea to have some one-on-one time with all of you, and I agree with him."

I pause for objections, but nobody says anything.

"I'd like to spend a few days meeting more closely with each of you individually. I'll spend that time asking about your process and noting other things that I see. I'll compile notes when I'm done with each person, then hopefully find ways where we can streamline things to make workloads feel a little lighter."

Quickly, I write a list of the order I'll go in, so I can give them each a heads up before we're done here.

"I also want to say, even though I've been mostly observing these last couple months, now that we have our team together, that will be changing. I want our first quarter of the year to be strong and for us to feel prepared for the spring releases we have scheduled. I know our department doesn't handle the releases directly, but without our editing, they wouldn't happen. Let's show the other departments how efficiently we can work and maybe get ahead of schedule before summer rolls around."

I pause and take a deep breath. Speaking with a smaller group is much easier than being the center of attention in a room full of mostly strangers.

"So, without further delay, this is the order I'd like to go in when working with each of you. I'll start with Piper, then Brian, Shannon, Michelle, Mikey, and Kasey. I'm going to start tomorrow instead of at the beginning of the week so that we can spend some time together, have the weekend for a break, and resume on Monday. Does this work for everyone?"

Every editor nods in agreement except for Piper. I'm sure she didn't expect to have to be alone with me, but the more she resists acknowledging me, the more I'm drawn to her. Her nervousness tells me I'm not the only one who felt something the other night. That draws me to her more, even though I know I shouldn't allow anything more to happen.

Now, I can't imagine not at least trying to connect with Piper to see what might happen. Nothing like a little forbidden romance to start the year off right.

I grab my things and push my chair back from the table. "That's it for today. Please feel free to come see me if you have any questions, and don't forget to think about the amount of submissions you believe you can get through in a week based on our new changes."

Everyone begins to get up, and Piper is nearly out the door when I call her name. Slowly, she turns back to me, letting strands of her long hair hide her face just like she had yesterday morning.

"Yes?" Her voice is smooth and sure, but the white on her knuckles where she's squeezing her notepad gives away her true feelings.

"Would you like to meet in my office or yours tomorrow morning?" I ask casually while grabbing my things and standing so I can step closer to her.

Her throat bobs before she answers. "Mine would be better if you want to see my process."

"Agreed. What time would you like me to join you?" I

step forward, and she moves further away from me until her back presses against the door.

"Eight would be fine with me." She pauses and stands a little taller before continuing. "How long will you be observing me each day?"

The room has mostly cleared. I'm tempted to mess with her, but I don't want to push her away so quickly.

"Only for a short time in the mornings these next two days, then maybe an afternoon on the third day if that works with your schedule." I raise an inquisitive brow, towering slightly over her maybe five-and-a-half-foot frame.

I expect her to cower back even more, but she surprises me by lifting her chin and meeting my steady gaze head on.

"Absolutely. I'll see you tomorrow, then, Mr. Adamson." Piper spins on her three-inch heel, and I watch her sweet ass walk out of the room.

My dick begins to harden. Half because of the way she addressed me and half from watching her go.

Damn it. Maybe I hadn't thought this through properly.

Alone time with Piper Fitz could be dangerous, but if she wants to pretend nothing happened, I'll play along.

For now.

Chapter Seven

DELICIOUSLY WRITTEN PORN

Piper

COLIN HAS STARTED A GAME HE'S NOT GOING TO win. I don't know what he's up to, but whatever it is, I'm not falling into his trap. No freaking way. At least, that's what I kept telling myself while I changed outfits four times this morning.

First, it was a red dress that made me look like a prostitute. Then, I somehow managed to overcompensate and turned myself into my grandmother by donning an ankle-length skirt and long-sleeved blouse. Next, I tried to be more business-oriented and still failed. Well, halfway. The slacks made my ass look perfect, but the matching shirt screamed "look at my boobs!" Not the message I was trying to present with my clothes. At least not consciously...

Now that I'm in my office, wearing a skirt that hangs loosely at mid-thigh and a black blouse that's neckline plunges a little lower than is probably appropriate for work, I feel like maybe I've already lost.

But then, Colin walks into my office while I'm standing

at my filing cabinet grabbing folders, and he has to pick his jaw up off the floor before he's able to speak.

"Good morning, Ms. Fitz," he says with a bit of a stammer in his voice.

I stand and face him while offering a sweet smile. "Good morning. Have a seat. I was just getting organized for the day."

When I expect him to sit on the opposite side of the desk, he surprises me by pulling the chair around to position himself only a foot away from me.

I do my best not to react to his closeness, and when I sit and meet his heady stare, there's a spark of mischief there.

I groan internally as I turn back to my computer. I'm not meant for games. There's no way I'm going to survive working this closely to Colin without saying something about New Year's Eve at some point. Maybe not right this second.

At least, I hope not.

"So, what's first on the agenda?" he asks, and I have to squeeze my thighs tighter together.

Seriously. What is wrong with American women when it comes to foreign accents? Especially when the guy is hot, the accent is like sprinkles on an already delicious sundae. Just not freaking fair.

I pick up my pen and roll it between my fingers more than necessary as I try to find the words I want to use.

"I have a to-do list that I create every Monday. When I get into the office, I take a look at that and my email to make sure nothing has changed priorities, then I dive into the most pertinent file," I say with as much professionalism as I can muster when his heat is beginning to brand my skin.

Stupid skirt. I don't know why I thought this was a good choice in attire.

Oh, yeah. Because I didn't think the sexy bastard was going to be sitting right next to me. For multiple hours *and* several days.

"What if you're not in the mood?" he asks with a deeper tenor to his words.

I gulp and slowly peek over at him. There's a darker ring around his light-gray eyes that holds me captive for one too many seconds. "The mood?" I finally ask.

He nods and—thankfully—leans a little further back in his chair. "When I was editing full-time, I had to be in the mood for certain genres in order to give the author my best work. I'm just wondering if your mind is the same."

Clearly, not.

"All of the genres that I'm given to work on are ones I enjoy, so it hasn't been a problem. I guess if it became one, I'd have to figure something out." The thought makes my stomach churn. I couldn't imagine not enjoying what I do.

"Very well." He reaches for the pad of paper I didn't even realize he'd set on the corner of my desk and pulls a pencil from his inner suitcoat pocket.

I try to see what he's writing, but I can't glean a damn thing, thanks to the muscled arm in my line of sight.

Maybe if I pretend he's not here, this will go a lot better.

I swivel my chair to face my computer screen and bring up my email. While that loads, I grab my to-do list and give it a quick once-over.

There are three books in my queue to be edited. One is a development edit for an author named Gina who I've only worked with once before, but not for edits. Then, the other two are line edits for authors I've only ever heard of.

So far, communication between me and each of them has been easy, but I can't deny that every time I send constructive notes back to the authors, I wonder how much they'll hate me.

A lot of them can't handle being told their book babies aren't perfect, which I get. They pour their hearts and souls into these beasts, and someone saying it's not right has to cut straight to the bone. That fear is the very reason I haven't finished writing a single manuscript. Even if I eventually do...I doubt I'll ever be as brave as these authors to share my work.

Gina promised me she has thick skin and asked that I really tear the book apart, so I've been a little more straightforward with hers. I just hope she wasn't lying and my thoughts don't ruin her day when I finally send them.

Outside of the edits, I also have communications with agents that I need to respond to, followed by new submissions to sort through.

"What's that?" Colin asks, and I jump in my seat.

Shit. I'd actually almost forgotten he was in the room.

His hand flinches as if he wants to reach for me, but at the last second stops and settles it back on the desk. "Sorry. I didn't mean to scare you."

I ignore his apology. "What's what?"

He points to my computer screen, and my eyes follow. "Is an author giving you problems?"

There's an email toward the top that's titled "I love to hate you", and it's from Michael, a Sci-Fi romance author whose book I edited while I was working from home.

I click on the message and laugh when I read the first line.

Piper,

When I got your notes back, I deleted the email and told

my agent you had no clue what you were doing. She forwarded me her copy of the email and told me to read it again, have a good night's rest, and read the words for a third time before I decided to really hate you.

Well, I did decide.

I hate you for being right, but I love you for the same reason. Thank you for your insight and really taking the time to understand Mira and Flynn. Their story is so much better because you didn't pull any punches, but you also weren't an asshole which is appreciated by the way.

I look forward to sending you the next book and it's coming along nicely thanks to your advice.

All the best,

Michael Reeves

"Do you get emails like that often?" Colin asks, seeming to be genuinely curious.

I shrug and mark the email as unread, so I remember to go back and reply when I don't have an audience. "A few respond that way, but I've only been doing this for six months now. I think Michael's was the fourth book I edited."

Colin's pencil taps against the pad of paper still in his grip. "Hopefully nobody is ever disrespectful or inappropriate when replying."

I let out an awkward chuckle. "Hasn't happened yet, but I'm sure it will someday. Hazards of the job."

"Of course, but that doesn't mean you have to put up with them." His mouth turns down. "You should tell me if anyone ever crosses a line they shouldn't, and I'll handle the situation myself."

The protective tone in his words does funny things to my stomach. I'm sure he doesn't mean them to sound heroic, but hell, I can't help hearing them that way or watching the way his mouth moves while he speaks and wondering what other things he might be able to elicit from me...

"So, what's next?" he finally asks, interrupting my wayward thoughts.

With a sigh—mostly from frustration with myself—I turn back to my computer. "You get to watch me take notes and read the emails I've received since yesterday."

"Great." He moves his chair another inch closer.

I think this man is trying to kill me with his presence. Seriously, if he gets any closer, I just might die. Then, my headstone would read some bullshit like "Here lies Piper Lucille Fitz. A hot mess who died from sexual tension."

Yeah, Kenzie would absolutely do something like that to me. Maybe I should think about a will... Might not be a bad idea.

First, I have to survive these meetings with Colin.

How can he act as if everything is completely normal after the way we dry humped each other on the dance floor and how intimately our tongues became acquainted?

Maybe it's a British thing. Maybe kissing and dancing isn't a big deal to them.

Or maybe he'd had more to drink than I realized and has no clue that we kissed.

Oh, God. What if I say something and he thinks I'm a psycho?

That alone is enough for me to force the memory of New Year's night to the dark recesses of my mind and focus on work like I'm supposed to be doing.

There are a few emails from agents I've never heard of, soliciting their author's books to me. Most of them won't ever see the light of day, but at Alliteration we try to give the benefit of the doubt for new submissions.

I forward all of those emails to the reader group email. They're our first line of defense for books and agents we don't currently have a relationship with, a Godsend that takes hours of work out of my week. They sort through them and prioritize chapters however needed. I'm rather thankful I don't have to worry about that process.

"Do you think the process for submissions works efficiently?" Colin asks, staring right into my eyes when I turn back to him.

My breath hitches, and it takes a second longer to answer than I would like. "I don't really know any different, so I'm not sure. I don't feel like we're constantly late on anything, which tells me that something is working."

He raises a brow. "But?"

"But there's nothing wrong with change, either. I guess we'll find out once you're done sitting with each of us."

Colin says nothing more, and I go back to doing my job as best I can, considering his nearness. The bounce of his knee, the intensity of his stare, even when it's not directly on me, the smell of his woodsy aftershave... All of it is like sensory overload, but I manage to get the rest of my morning things completed before opening Gina's manuscript.

You've got to be fucking kidding me.

How could I have done this to myself? No, the fates couldn't be that cruel.

The comment I last left marks where I ended and is right at the start of a sex scene. Am I really going to read deliciously written porn with this attractive man next to me?

Absolutely not. If I thought I was going to die sitting next to him, I might explode from the expertly detailed sex scene that awaits me.

His thick cock pulsates inside her tight pussy...

Dear lord. What am I doing right now?

I needed to focus, and not on sex or how attracted I am to the one man in this city I can't have.

Yes, I can do that. I have to.

What the hell was I doing before? Oh, yeah. Bypassing the porn. Right.

Given Colin doesn't know my process, I quickly scroll past my comment and find myself at the start of another chapter that isn't nearly as awkward to read.

He points his pen at the screen. "There were several pages without comments. Does that happen often?"

Shit. I have no idea how to answer that and take a drink of my water while I flounder for words.

"Some scenes I like to marinate on. Give them a read through and then come back to them once I've finished the rest of the book. Helps my notes incorporate the bigger picture, you know?"

For a total lie, it isn't half-bad. I mean I do go back to some notes and leave more details about how I felt in the moment and then once the book was done, but I don't ever skip entire scenes like that.

Colin makes more notes, and I begin my job. Quickly, I'm immersed in a fantasy world filled with epic magic, detailed world-building, and suspense that has all other thoughts in my mind vanishing by the line I consume.

I'm several notes and a dozen pages in before Colin taps me on the shoulder and nearly gives me a heart attack.

My hand covers my chest, and I turn toward him. He's much closer than I expected, and my eyes fall directly to his lips. My tongue darts out, wetting my own, and I take a deep inhale. Our proximity makes my heart race and I'm not even sure what's happening.

"Piper?" His eyes rove over me, branding my skin everywhere they go.

"Huh? I mean, sorry. You scared me. I kind of forgot you were here again," I stammer and attempt to move further away from him, but I'm blocked in by my desk.

His hand reaches forward and pushes a hair back that was stuck to my lip. "I see that. Maybe I should come back this afternoon when you're through some of those chapters?"

"I'll be doing this all day. I don't know how informative observing me will be until I'm done with the book," I say, trying not to melt in my seat from his closeness.

He finally backs up. "Very well. I don't want to be overly intrusive. When will you be done with the book?"

I laugh without meaning to. "Done, done? Or done with this read-through and set of comments?"

His head cocks to the side. "Both."

Since he doesn't seem to know how I was trained, I detail my plans for this book. "I'll be done with my first round of comments late today, as long as no fires pop up. Then, I'll print the book, take it home, and make more additions with a slower read-through. After that, I'll add everything to the electronic copy and send that to the author. Then, I'm done until they have questions or are ready for line edits."

He frowns. "Do you always take the books home to work after hours?"

"When I was working from home and wasn't with my friends, I'd find myself picking up the books to keep working. I truly enjoy what I do, so it doesn't always feel like work, if that makes sense."

Colin reaches for his notepad and buttons the front of

his suit, now that he's standing. "Makes perfect sense. I'll see you tomorrow, Piper."

As he walks out of my office, shutting the door behind him, I fall back into my chair.

Why did that last bit feel like a threat instead of a confirmation?

Chapter Eight

PENIS READY

Colin

Fuck. I was only at Piper's desk for a little over an hour, and my cock is hard as a rock while walking back to my office. I'd thought pushing her buttons would be fun, but the idea has completely backfired on me.

At least my time with Piper won't be just for my torture. It should also be good for the team, if I can survive the first few days being so close to that alluring woman. Getting to know the other editors' processes will help to streamline the way we do things now that everyone is together, but... Shit. Maybe I should have saved being so close to Piper for last.

Well, it's too late for that now.

Once I'm logged into my computer, I see that I have an email from Steve. He wants an update on how my meeting went yesterday. A bit annoying that he doesn't trust me to handle my staff, but I reply anyway, detailing my plans for the next several weeks.

By the time I'm done typing the email, I feel better

about the whole situation. Yes, being around Piper is difficult, but the main purpose behind all of this should work swimmingly.

I might not be the most social person, but I know how to supervise and get shit done. This will be the best way to garner respect from those who haven't been in the office and to cement the relationships I've already been building with the others.

I go about my day, and before I know it, it's more than half over. I've been going through emails from some of the readers about potential manuscripts and assigning them to the other editors for another pass before we make official offers on anything.

"Your toasted chicken sandwich, Colin," Sandy, the department assistant, says as she hands me a white bag.

The smell of toasted focaccia bread fills my senses, and I groan. "I didn't realize I was hungry until you walked in. Thanks for bringing this to me."

She smiles and brushes a few strands of silver hair behind her left ear. "Do you need anything else?"

I'm already opening the bag when I say, "No. Thank you for asking."

She disappears without another word, and I let out a happy sigh. One of the biggest adjustments when I first moved here was the food. I've slowly gotten used to the greasier and heavier style cooking, but when I found a sandwich shop that uses focaccia bread, I nearly wept with joy.

The bread is still warm from being toasted, and I quickly take my first bite. With my mouth full, I reach for a napkin before the special sauce they use can drip down my chin.

As I'm cleaning my face, my boss Steve walks in. "Lunch time, eh?"

I nod and swallow a bite that should have been chewed a bit longer. "Seems like it."

He leans against my doorframe, and I'm slightly grateful he's not getting too comfortable. "I know I already came by this morning, and I don't want to sound like a broken record or an overbearing boss, but after reading your email, I just wanted to come convey in person how glad I was to read your plans. I'll admit that I was worried for a while when you remained stand-offish. Alliteration is all about working as a team that's actually more of a family, and we want you to be front and center of the editors. So, thank you for stepping up now that you have your whole group under you, and please know we appreciate the efforts you're making now."

I want to ask if he thought I wasn't making an effort before, but I hold my tongue. As long as he's happy now, I don't need to dredge up the past.

"Glad to hear it," I say since I'm not sure what he expects from me. His managing tactics aren't anything I've worked with before.

"Alright. Well, I'll let you get back to things. Let me know if you need anything from me. In the meantime, I'll back off while you're getting to know your team."

Nothing would make me happier, I think but definitely don't say out loud.

I take another bite of my lunch and wave as he walks out.

Now, if only I could figure out how to handle this situation with Piper, things would be dandy.

THE FOLLOWING DAY, I GET THE EMAIL I'VE BEEN anticipating from Piper. She's done with her first round of edits on the manuscript she's been working on, so it's time for me to return to her office to see how she handles the next steps.

My heart speeds up, and I place my hands on the metal desktop in front of me. I take a deep breath to get my shit together. I shouldn't be this smitten with a woman after having only kissed her. I don't know what's wrong with me, but something has to change.

Maybe it's time I said something to her. Lay everything out instead of pretending that night didn't happen.

The more I think about that option, the more I think it's the best solution, but that doesn't make it any easier after having worked with her and kept my mouth shut.

Then again, she hasn't said anything, either.

I grab my notepad and pencil, then give my head a solid shake. "I'm a grown man. I can talk about kissing a woman and not lose my shit."

Without allowing myself to continue overthinking, I open my door and head toward Piper's. She's only four doors down from me, and I'm there in mere seconds.

Her office is open, and I hear music playing softly from inside.

When I step through the doorway, her head is bobbing and her lips are moving, but no words are coming out. I smile, observing her without her knowing, and something warms inside me.

Damn it. I can't do this. She's my employee. One I'm not allowed to date, according to the legal documents I signed when I took this job. I know I said I didn't care before, but that was possibly an understatement.

I knock on the frame, and her head jerks toward me. "Oh. I didn't think you'd be here so quickly."

My palms are sweaty, and I switch the notepad to my other hand before answering. "You said you were done. I thought I'd head right over so you weren't left waiting. Do you need more time?"

She shakes her head and pushes back in her chair. "No, you're fine. Have a seat."

I close the door behind me this time. Normally, I would prefer it open because people like to talk about what they don't know, but if I'm going to have a much-needed conversation with this woman, then I don't want anyone to overhear.

The thought occurs to me that I could ask her to meet me after work, but I dismiss it quickly. That would only be asking for more problems if someone saw us.

Piper eyes the closed door before turning back to her computer screen. "Do you want to see every step, like how I print the pages, or just the overall process?"

I grin. "I'm not a micromanager, Piper. The overall process is great, but if there are any details you learned from your previous coworkers you think I should know, then please speak about those as well."

Instead of sitting next to Piper like before, I remain on the other side of the desk and set my things down. She makes a humming noise in her throat and starts clicking her mouse. I might not want to be a micromanager, but I sure as hell enjoy watching her work.

The way her lips thin and head tilts slightly to the right while she's going through the settings before hitting print. Or how she tosses her chestnut hair out of her way, and it falls in soft waves down her back.

She turns toward me, and I know she's caught me

appraising her, but I don't jerk my gaze away. Instead, I say, "Would you like me to get the pages for you?"

She swallows thickly and shakes her head. "I'll be back in a minute."

While she's gone, I take the time to check out the things she's brought into the office. On her desk, the first thing I notice is a picture frame with her and two other women inside. They're wearing dresses, and the sky is blue behind them. A glow shines over all three, but it's Piper's face I can't tear my gaze away from.

Her skin seems to glow from the sun beaming down on them, and her smile is bright. She appears more at ease there than even how I saw her in the nightclub.

I force my eyes closed and turn my head before reopening them. I can't stare. I can't touch. I can't want. Piper Fitz is supposed to be off limits, and I need to repeat that as many times as necessary for the truth of that statement to set in.

At least, that's what I should do.

She enters back into the room, and I try not to look at her arse in the gray slacks she's wearing. I try and fail.

The big stack of papers in her hands settles onto the desk with an audible thud. "Do you have your penis ready?"

My mouth pops open, but no words exit for too many awkward seconds. "Excuse me?"

She points to my paper and pencil. "Are you ready to take notes?"

There's no flush to her cheeks. No stutter to her words. The only thing off with her face is the crease between her brows at my confusion.

Am I fucking hearing things, or does she have no idea she said *penis* instead of pencil just now?

Piper takes a step toward me. "Are you okay, Colin?"

I glance back at the door and make sure she closed it on her way back in.

"Do you remember me from New Year's Eve?" I blurt out, because if I don't, I just might go crazy.

Now, it's her turn to flounder and flush. The pink on her cheeks reminds me of that night, and it takes every restraint inside me not to push her against the office wall and devour that mouth of hers once again.

Bloody hell, this was a bad idea.

Chapter Nine

BASICALLY SCREWED

Piper

I DON'T KNOW IF I WANT TO BE MAD THAT HE remembers me and hasn't said anything or grateful, because the awkwardness that's settling in around us is way worse than the tension we were previously wading in.

Before I answer him, I take my seat, needing the desk between us for this conversation. "Yes, Colin. I remember you."

His fingers drum over his raised knee and his face is unreadable, which puts me on edge, so I start to ramble to fill the silence.

"I didn't know who you were that night. I wasn't trying to put you in a bad position or anything. It was just kissing and some dancing. Basically nothing," I say while my hands twist together underneath my desk.

As soon as the word "nothing" leaves my lips, Colin's eyes heat and stare me down. "Nothing? I'd love to know what you consider *something*."

Shit. Now he must think I'm a whore or something from the way he said that.

My eyes drift to the closed door. What if someone walked in without knocking? What if the other employees are already wondering why I'm in here alone with our boss? Damn it. This isn't at all how I pictured my first week in this office.

Colin smooths his palms over the sleek surface of the desk and lets out a deep breath. "Listen, Piper. I didn't mean to offend you or take you by surprise. I just couldn't pretend any longer."

"It's fine. At least it's been mentioned now. We both know what we did, and we know it can't happen again," I say, assuming that's the point he's trying to make.

He nods and slowly pulls his hands back to his lap. "Yes, we know what happened that night. I just needed to be sure I wasn't the only one who remembered."

He didn't specifically say that the kiss couldn't happen again. Why? Why didn't he confirm what I said?

More importantly, why does that excite me so damn much?

"I like to think I know my limits enough to prevent me from forgetting the things I do, even while I've been drinking," I say, unsure if I'm defending myself or trying to make light of a very uncomfortable situation. Maybe a little of both.

Colin smirks and picks up his pencil. "Or maybe I'm just unforgettable."

I bark out a laugh and have to hold my stomach as the muscles ache from the unexpected action. When my bout of laughter finishes, I see him frowning at me and realize he wasn't joking.

My shoulders straighten, and I turn to my computer screen. "I'm sorry. This really isn't a conversation we should be having. Given nothing else can happen, we just need to keep that night where it belongs, in the past."

I don't look at him again, but I can feel his gaze locked on me. My eyes are focused hard on the screen, but I can't see any of the words there. Shit. Why couldn't he have left things as they were? I would have gotten over wondering if he remembered, and we could have worked together without any weirdness.

Now that I know he remembers, I'm not sure how I'm supposed to proceed, especially with how freaking quiet he's being.

Once the tightening in my chest can't take anymore, I reach for my folder that I keep for each author I'm working with. Inside is a checklist that I know by heart since it's the one I used as an assistant before, but still, it holds me accountable for each and every task.

I pull the sheet out and set it next to the manuscript. I begin going down the list, marking off things I've already completed and lightly circling what's next with the intention of explaining that to Colin just as soon as I'm done, but before I can finish, he stands and leans over the desk, towering over me. His darkening eyes bore into me.

"I don't want to make you uncomfortable, and it seems you have a process that doesn't allow you to speak much. Perhaps this was a poor decision on my part." I wonder *which* decision he deems poor, but he's so close that I can feel his breath on my face and can't seem to form words.

I want to squirm in my chair, but I manage to finally get my thoughts together and stay perfectly still. "I was filling this out and then I was going to share it with you. I didn't think you wanted me to narrate you through everything I was doing."

There's a challenge in my tone that I've never used with a supervisor before. We lock stares, and it's a battle of wills in the making. I won't break first. I can't. Not after everything he just said, and even the stuff he didn't say.

I promised myself that I would do things differently this year, that I would embody all that I learned from my friends and about myself over the last decade of adulthood.

My chin juts out a little further, and I place my hands over one another on the desk, then lick my lips without thinking the action through.

Colin's eyes dart toward my mouth, and he moves in closer, using his height to his advantage and entering my personal space.

"I'm going to walk away now, Piper," is all he says before turning around and exiting my office, closing the door softly behind him.

I sink back into my chair, let my eyes flutter closed, and release a heavy breath from between my lips. "What the hell am I supposed to do with that?"

My hands rub over my face, then I reopen my eyes to find hundreds of pages that need to be gone through. Pages that include all the angst I'm currently feeling.

———

Thanks to today's earlier fiasco in my office, it took longer than I care to admit for my brain to concentrate well enough to begin my second round of edits on Gina's book.

Even though I could have taken the pages home, I

already had everything strewn about my desk, and trying to recreate my process at home seemed like too much work after the day I'd had. So, when I peek at the clock and realize it's after nine in the evening, I finally decide to call it quits for the day.

Though, I don't mind putting in the extra hours. Not when I don't have any other plans for the weekend and am truly enjoying the fantasy book. It needs some finessing, but what first draft doesn't?

I organize all the pages I've already read through and place them in the folder before sliding everything into my bag to take home. I have no doubts I'll get bored and decide to work again over the weekend.

Once everything is as picked up as it's going to get, I head out my door and to the elevator. There are still a few office lights on, and I smile, thankful I'm not the only person with nothing better to do on a Friday night.

Just as the doors close, a hand reaches through, and they open back up. I move to the side so I'm not in someone else's way, then freeze when I realize it isn't just any other employee who's entered the elevator with me.

Colin's eyes go wide when he sees me, and I can at least breathe a little easier knowing he hadn't been creepily watching and waiting for me to leave so he could follow.

He slowly enters, then presses the button to close the door faster while still looking at me. "I hope you don't mind sharing the lift."

My shoulders shrug, and I hold my bag tighter in front of me. "I don't own the *lift*."

Colin grins, and my stomach aches from how attractive I find the dimples on his cheeks as he does.

"Working late?" he asks, and I snort.

"I fell asleep at my desk," I joke, but he doesn't catch my humor.

He whips his head in my direction. "You what?"

I pat his shoulder and laugh. "Kidding, Colin. Yes, I was working late."

"Me, too."

"I didn't figure you were sleeping in your office," I tease. When he chuckles at my comment, the knot that's been weighing on my chest since he walked away earlier loosens some.

Then, he does something I don't expect because this isn't supposed to happen in real life. That sexy man hits the stop button on the elevator, and we come to a jerking halt.

My back is suddenly pressed against the metal wall, and my free hand is gripping the handle there much too tightly. "Why did you do that?"

"Because the thought of you running away from me once those doors open to the parking garage was too much for my mind to handle. I needed to apologize," he says, stepping forward and right into my personal space.

"I didn't mean to... Whatever happened earlier, that's not how I wanted things to go," he says, now dangerously close to me.

My chest expands, and I look up at him with hooded eyes. "It's okay."

His head shakes, and he lifts a hand until the back of his fingers are brushing against my warm cheek. "No, it's not. I had intentions of returning to that club to find you again, but then I saw you here at Alliteration and I didn't know how to handle knowing that you were supposed to be off limits, so I wanted to get closer to you to see if you felt anything. When I thought you didn't remember, I acted poorly. I'm sorry."

He's apologizing to *me*? Well, I didn't expect that, especially when I didn't think either of us had done anything wrong. At least, not yet.

"It's really okay, Colin. I promise." I release the handle behind me and adjust the bag in my arms, fully expecting him to take a step back, but when he doesn't, I get lost in his stare once again.

There is a darkening flicker in his eyes that holds me captive. There's nothing I can do other than stand there, holding my things tightly to my chest so that I don't do something like grab his neck and drag him closer until our lips connect.

"Piper," he says gruffly.

"Colin," I reply as a whisper.

He reaches for the protective shield that is my bag and sets it on the ground, never removing his eyes from mine as he does.

My chest rises and falls rapidly, and fireworks are exploding inside my stomach. I desperately want him to touch me. I want to feel his lips on mine and have him pressed against me.

God, I want that so badly. But he's supposed to be off limits. He's my boss.

I can't want him.

I can't have him.

I can't...

Before I can finish the thought, his head bends closer, and I find myself rising on my toes to meet him in the middle. When his lips touch mine once, twice, and a third time, I throw all caution to the wind and grip his suitcoat with both hands.

"Just as sweet as I remembered," he murmurs against my lips.

My body melts against his hard chest, and I hold on tighter to him. One of his hands wraps around the back of my neck while the other goes to my lower back, pressing me closer.

Mother fuck… He's hard as a rock, and if only I was a few inches taller, he'd be positioned perfectly.

Even still, a moan escapes me. Colin's fingers dig into my heated skin at the sound, and he inches impossibly closer to me.

The smolder inside me is quickly turning into an inferno, making me forget all the reasons I should not have my tongue halfway down this particular man's throat.

"Is anyone in there?" a crackle of a voice echoes around us.

It's a stark reminder that we're still in the stopped elevator. At work. A place that says we can't date. I jerk away from Colin, but my bracelet gets stuck on a button from his shirt, and I move back closer to untangle the silver, but so does Colin. Our heads collide when he bends down too quickly to help.

"Ouch," I groan and pull back, but then I trip over my bag that I forget is on the ground and end up on my ass, with a bleeding wrist and a piece of Colin's shirt dangling from my bracelet.

Can this get any worse? God, I hope not.

Colin presses the call button. "Yeah, sorry. I tripped and hit the stop button. Didn't know how to get it to go again."

"Uh, you could have read the directions next to the stop button, but I'll reset it for you, man," the same voice says.

My hand covers my mouth as I hold back my laugh and simultaneously try not to cry from how badly this has gone. Maybe it's a sign I should be heeding…

"Shit," Colin mutters before responding, "Thanks, mate."

The voice doesn't come back, and I'm thankful as hell that there are no cameras in these elevators.

My wrist stings badly from the white gold digging into my skin when I fell back. At least it didn't break.

There's only a faint layer of blood. Still, I start trying to take the bracelet off, so my skin doesn't get further irritated.

Colin bends down and gently pushes my hand away. "I'm sorry. Again."

"That wasn't really your fault," I say breathily as he undoes the clasp and inspects my wrist.

"I invaded your personal space without asking for permission and kissed you when we both know I shouldn't have. I'd say even if you didn't want to push me away, this is definitely my fault." By the time he finishes speaking, there's a grin on his face and he's tucking my bracelet into the side pocket of my bag that's still under my knees from when I fell.

He further rips his light gray dress shirt and wraps a strip of fabric around my injury. "Shirt was done for anyway," he says with a shrug, then helps me back up.

The elevator doors open to the parking garage below the building, and I reach down to grab my bag, except Colin already has it in his hands.

"Do you mind if I walk you to your car?" he asks, full of politeness I'm not sure what to do with.

"Sure. I mean no, I don't mind." Damn it. Why is the answer to "do you mind" anything always so confusing?

Instead of calling me out on my stumbling words, Colin's hand presses against my lower back. I lead the way to my car while trying not to die from the heat searing into my spine from his touch.

Why did he have to kiss me again? We could have just swept all of this into a dark corner and kept things simple.

Now, there's a niggle of a thought at the center of my mind that says nothing with Colin is going to be simple. The way that thought excites me... Well, I'm basically screwed.

Chapter Ten

STUPID FUCKING SPIDER

Colin

KISSING PIPER AGAIN LAST NIGHT PROBABLY wasn't my brightest idea, but when the same spark as before ignited between the two of us, I knew I'd made the right choice.

She is smart and beautiful and kind and thoughtful. I might not know her as well as I'd like, but I've learned those things this week while watching her at work. Now that it's Saturday, the thought of waiting until Monday to see her again is sitting in my stomach like soured milk.

Given she's my employee, I should go out and find someone else to distract my thoughts, but instead, I do exactly what I shouldn't and head into my home office to log onto my laptop.

Am I going to regret my actions later? Possibly. Do I give a single fuck in the moment? Absolutely not.

I google "Piper Fitz" in hopes of finding something about her online, but unfortunately, I don't remember where she moved from. I have no way to find that out without going through her employee file, which I could do as her boss, but my stomach churns at the thought.

I'm already crossing enough lines by wanting her. I don't need to make matters worse by being a stalker as well.

I do, however, have access to her phone number as her supervisor. I could call or even send a text, but again, I don't want to overstep. I don't want to pressure her.

But fuck, if I don't want *her*.

My cat Charlie makes a God-awful sound I'm sure is supposed to be a meow but doesn't hit the mark. Then, he jumps up on my desk and waltzes in front of my screen as if this is his domain.

"Bugger off, furball." I gently push him away, but he circles back around. "Seriously, cat. I will find you a new home."

I wouldn't really. Somehow, I've grown fond of the fluff. Maybe it's because I've felt alone in this big city ever since I moved here and talking to him is better than talking to myself, but I'm not in the mood to analyze my sanity.

"Sir Charles, move your arse," I demand.

He flicks his long tail up, lets out a short meow, then hops down. High-maintenance, cheeky bastard.

When he's out of my way, I click through a few social media sites just in case I get lucky, but when I don't find anything, I decide I need to do something to release some of this pent-up energy before I stop listening to reason.

I lean back in my chair and glance out the window. It's still early enough. I could go for a run. Maybe clear my head a bit at the same time.

As much as I don't feel like a workout, a few laps around the neighborhood could be exactly what I need.

AN HOUR LATER, MY PHONE IS DEAD, SO I HAVE NO more music to drown out my thoughts, which maybe isn't the worst thing. As I'm making my way back to my house, I think only about Piper.

Ignoring the fact that she's my employee, I know that I want her and, after last night in the lift, I know she wants me as well, regardless of the fine print in our contracts.

I tried to convince myself that I should fight whatever feelings are between us, but I quickly decide that I can't. Not any longer. As soon as Monday comes, I'll ask her if we can get together outside of work, and I'll tell her how I feel. She might tell me to piss off, but she might not.

I don't know her well enough to be sure, but I hope to change that soon.

With my mind made up, I head in the direction of home while trying to enjoy the sounds of the city. It's working until I hear someone scream in the fenced yard I've just passed.

Then, there's a squeal followed by a low, "Die, you bastard."

Not my problem. I need to keep jogging. The city is full of crazy people. Even still, I find myself pausing to find out if I should consider calling the police.

"What the hell are you doing, Pipe? And why is everything dark?" another woman's voice sounds, but this one sounds like it's coming from a phone.

"Let me just make sure it's dead," someone replies in a voice I've recently become familiar with.

I shouldn't be here. I shouldn't stop to listen. I shouldn't ask if everything is okay. I really bloody shouldn't.

My feet carry me to the fence, taking charge even

though my thoughts say otherwise. "Is everyone okay over there?" I ask without peeking over the fence.

"You've got to be shitting me," Piper mutters, not so quietly.

"Don't tell me you have a hot British boss *and* neighbor. Seriously, if I wasn't in a relationship, I'd—"

"Shut up, Kenzie," Piper hisses, then I can hear her footfalls but can't tell which direction they're going.

A grin rises on my face while I wait. She knows I'm here. There's no point in leaving unless she asks me to.

I expect her to come to the fence, but then I hear a door slide open and close. Okay. Maybe I should leave.

Just as I step back to the sidewalk with my back to her house, I hear my name called. I turn around to find a very upset Piper glaring at me from the corner of the sidewalk.

"What are you doing here?" she demands.

My hands go up innocently, and I stay put. "I was out for a walk. I heard someone scream. I didn't know it was you. Not at first. I was just leaving."

Her brow raises pointedly. "So, you didn't have my address and come spy on me?"

I mean, I'd thought about it earlier, but now, I'm glad I hadn't misused the information I could have gotten from work. I'm not sure she would have forgiven me for that one, considering how pissed she seems with her crossed arms and bouncing bare foot.

"No, Piper. I had no idea you lived here." I nod toward the house next to us.

She rolls her eyes. "I live in the next one over. Come on."

My eyes widen as she turns to go back toward the houses. "You want me to follow you?"

"It's better than my neighbors hearing us talk," she says with a huff.

I decide not to ask any other questions and quicken my pace to catch up. She's wearing tight leggings and a loose green long-sleeve that makes her eyes stand out even more than usual. Her long chestnut strands are pulled up into a messy bun with a few longer pieces still trailing down her back.

She stomps through her front door, and I quietly follow, closing it behind me. As soon as we're both in the short hallway, Piper whirls around, catching me by surprise when she pokes a finger in my chest.

"You just had to make this complicated, didn't you? You couldn't let that night go. You had to say something and then kiss me again in that damn elevator. And now you're here? I don't get it, Colin. Did you not sign the same employment contract I did? Do you not realize that if we choose to continue whatever has been happening this week that one of us will get transferred or maybe even fired? And I'm sure I can bet on which one that is. Not their precious new editor-in-chief they brought in all the way from mother-freaking London!"

Her chest is heaving, her hands are now flailing in the air, and when she's done scolding me, she begins to pace right in front of me.

I reach for her, hoping to calm some of her agitation, but she smacks my hand. "Don't touch me."

That has my back pressed against the door and eyes widening. "I'm sorry, Piper. I'm aware of the rule about no dating within departments, but this was just a coincidence. I didn't follow you into the lift, and I never would have stopped if I hadn't heard the scream."

"Stupid fucking spider," she mutters before meeting my

stare again. "So, you're saying this is all just fate pushing us together, even though you're my boss?"

I'm tempted to smile, but I keep my face neutral to avoid further upsetting Piper. "I'm not saying anything other than things happened unintentionally. Well, except when I kissed you in the lift. I meant for that, but everything else just happened. Whether that be fate or something else, I don't know."

She throws her hands up and turns away from me. "Why is this happening to me?"

I'm certain I shouldn't answer that question, but I do at least follow her further into the house. If she doesn't kick me out, I don't intend to leave until we get a few more things sorted.

At least this time we won't be interrupted.

Chapter Eleven

I CALL BULLSHIT

Piper

THERE HASN'T BEEN A GUY IN MY LIFE IN YEARS. Sure, I've dated, but boyfriend material? Not since... Hell, I can't even remember. Two, maybe three years ago? Whatever. That doesn't matter. What *does* matter is the fact that Colin seems to be actually interested in me, and I maybe feel the same way about him, but he's still my mother-freaking boss.

That little detail hasn't changed, and I don't think it will anytime soon, regardless of how many times we're forced together.

I head to the kitchen, needing something to ease the craziness storming inside me. My teal-colored kettle catches my eye, and I fill it with water before placing it back on the stove. The burner turns on, and I stay facing the oven. I could get hot water from the coffee maker like normal, but this will take longer. I need the distraction right now.

My foot is tapping, and I can't unclench my hands. It isn't fair that things are so complicated. I know I said I wanted to live life more adventurously this year, but having sex with my boss isn't even close to what I meant by that.

Shit. Sex with him? No, I don't need to be thinking about that. Not now and not ever.

I hear Colin's footfalls enter the kitchen, and he pauses a moderate distance away from me. At least, it feels that way.

"Piper, can we talk about this?" he asks calmly.

I take a deep breath and consider my options. I could say fuck all the things and channel my inner Kenzie by doing what I want, which would be to let Colin take me right here on the counter, instead of what I should.

But then, what did that say about me? I might be trying to be more carefree, but am I willing to throw away everything I've worked for the last few years to do so?

No, I'm not, and that's our biggest problem.

Slowly, I swivel around to face him. I take in the stubble that's grown on his face since yesterday, the navy-blue jogging shorts, and the black t-shirt that hugs the muscles along his chest that I shouldn't be ogling. The man really is too attractive for his own good.

His gray eyes stare at me as I try to find the words I need to say.

With another steadying breath, I begin. "What's the point of talking about any of this, Colin? You're my boss. We are not allowed to date. Nothing more can happen between us. It doesn't matter if we feel anything for each other. I won't have everything I've worked for and given up to get here be thrown away because I wanted to get laid."

Colin takes a tentative step forward, moving until he's leaning against my counter. "So, if I wasn't your boss, then you'd go on a date with me?"

I can't stop from glaring at him, but the action isn't as

forceful as I'd like it to be. "Is that all you got out of what I just said?"

He gives his head a slight shake, and I see his lips twitch. "No, what I heard is that I was right about you. You're smart and strong and incredible. You're denying yourself what you want because that's the right thing to do. I wish I could say I was the same, but I've lived on this earth for nearly forty years, Piper. I can't help but want what I want."

He moved closer as he spoke and now stands just a few inches before me. His hand raises and fingers lightly graze the exposed skin on my collarbone.

"I respect you and your choices, but I can't walk away without saying everything that I need to. Is that okay?" he asks.

I want to say no because I know hearing whatever he's going to say isn't going to help our situation, but instead I find myself nodding. "Go ahead."

He drops his hand to his side before continuing. "I've been through enough to know that I don't want to walk away from the feelings I have for you, but I will if that's what you want. Before you decide that, though, what if we didn't ignore what's between us? What if we kept things private just to see where they end up? Maybe there's a solution we've yet to see here and we won't find it unless we try."

Kenzie's previous suggestion that maybe Colin would be willing to transfer departments instead comes back to me. Loudly.

Maybe there is a solution here, but I don't want to point out things neither of us are willing to commit to just yet. Hell, I don't even want to think about any "feelings." Even if there's a chance that things could work out, just seeing what happens between Colin and me seems too risky. I don't know if even the new Piper is capable of taking a leap like that, no matter how hard he makes my chest pound and how much I want to feel his body against mine again.

Damn this man for making me want things I haven't in years.

We've only kissed twice, and I've only talked to him a few times, but there is something about him that has me craving more of his kisses and wondering what his touch would feel like in places it doesn't belong.

The fact that he seems so certain about what he wants. How calm and in control he's been. How every word that leaves his lips seems to be well thought-out and meaningful. All of that nearly crumbles me.

Still, I'm not that person. I don't make rash decisions or throw caution to the wind. As much as I want to change, that isn't going to happen in a week.

"I need time to consider what I'm risking by saying yes. It won't be you who gets fired if we're caught. We both know that," I say with a tinge of sadness in my voice.

Colin cups my cheek and locks gazes with me. "I understand you don't know me, and you have no reason to trust me, but I promise, if you agree to see me and the wrong person finds out about us, I would quit before I let them fire you."

His warmth seeps into me, and I badly want to believe in the sincerity of his words. My chest tightens and skin tingles from the powerfulness of what he's said. While it helps, I still need more time. When I make my decision, I need to know that it isn't because my mind is clouded by my attraction to the sexy Brit standing in front of me.

"Thank you for saying that. It helps. Really," I say while consciously doing my best not to lean into his touch.

He nods. When I think he's going to drop his hand and step back, he moves closer. "Can I kiss you again, in case it's the last chance I get?"

Oh, hell. Seriously? How am I supposed to say no to *that*?

My head moves up and down ever so slightly, but he grins. "I need to hear a verbal confirmation, Piper. I won't take advantage of you."

Right, because he's a true gentleman and I'm an idiot for even thinking of telling him no.

"Kiss me, Colin." My words are hardly a whisper, but he doesn't miss them.

The distance between us closes. He wraps one hand around my waist, and the other goes behind my head. I barely have time to register my own actions before his tongue is sliding against my lips and I'm opening for him.

I hold on to his shirt for dear life and hope like hell that I'm not making matters worse by allowing this to happen again, especially when it feels like his lips are branding mine and there will be no way to ever forget this moment.

His tongue sweeps through my mouth, and I give back as much as he takes. A small moan builds in my throat, and I can't keep it down when his lower hand pushes against my back, causing my pussy to press right over his throbbing dick. Thin clothes aren't ideal in these kinds of situations.

Without realizing what I'm doing, I find myself inching forward, needing more contact between the two of us. More of his touch. Everywhere.

His mouth moves away from mine, down my neck and to my shoulder, where he places soft kisses on my skin before pulling back just enough to lean his forehead against mine.

Our ragged breaths combine, and I already miss his tongue.

"I'm going to go now, but please know, I really don't want to. It's just the right thing to do. Take as long as you need to make your decision, Piper. I'll wait for you." Colin kisses the tip of my nose, gives my hips a quick squeeze, then turns to exit the kitchen.

I stay pressed against the stove right where he left me and listen to his soft footsteps until I hear the door open and then close behind him with an audible click.

My hands rub over my face, and I try to calm my racing heart. I'm a grown-ass woman. Not some high-schooler who just had her first kiss. I shouldn't be this worked up.

Yet...I am.

Just when I finally feel like I've got my shit together, the whistle of the kettle sounds off, nearly giving me a heart attack and causing me to yelp.

I turn around and glare at the pot. "Not cool."

A moment passes when I consider pouring the steaming water down the sink, but tea still sounds good, so I grab a mug then a bag of chamomile to drape over the rim of the cup.

Carefully, I pour the hot liquid and carry my drink to the living room. After setting it on the table, I throw myself onto the couch and consider putting a pillow over my face so I can scream as loudly as I want.

Frustrated doesn't even begin to describe how I feel right now.

My eyes stare up at the white ceiling, and I try to consider my options, but nothing sounds right inside my head.

Colin said everything I could possibly want to hear, but can I trust him that much? Can I hinge everything on believing he'd attempt to protect me should things go awry?

Just when I'm about to give up on figuring out the answers I so desperately need, my phone pings with a text.

Ella: Sorry I couldn't make the video chat earlier. You guys busy now?

As I'm typing my reply, Kenzie chimes in first.

Kenzie: I'm still free, but hopefully Piper's not.

She adds eggplant and heart-eye emojis to emphasize her point, and I groan loudly, deleting my text then doing my best to defend myself.

Ella: What? With who? Her boss??

Piper: Nothing happened. We talked, he left.

Kenzie: I call BULLSHIT.

A video chat starts ringing through.

Damn it. I can't lie to their faces, even if it's through my camera. I'm tempted not to answer, but that will only give Kenzie more ammunition to keep prodding at me.

I connect, and they're both already on the screen. I wave at Ella. "How was dinner?"

She shakes her head. "We're not here to talk about me. Tell me why the hot English guy was at your house and what the hell happened?"

Kenzie waggles her brows. "Yeah, Piper. Tell her before I give my version."

With a heavy sigh, I recount the screaming, thanks to the stupid spider that was on my leg, then Colin hearing me and asking if everything was okay before ending with everything that happened in the kitchen. Well, almost everything.

They both listen intently, staying quiet and nodding or grimacing at appropriate times.

"Did anything happen between you two before he left?" Ella asks once I'm done.

I bite my lip and nod. "He asked if he could kiss me, and I might have said yes."

Kenzie's eyes go wide. "He asked? Like for permission? Oh, man. That's...kinda hot."

The hand not holding my phone up covers my face. "I. Know."

"One thing I want you to remember is while you've worked your ass off to get where you are—and we're so proud of you for that—your happiness is still very important. You might enjoy what you're doing for Alliteration, but those books aren't going to keep you warm at night. If there's any chance Colin could be *the* guy for you, then I think you need to take the risk."

The words leave Kenzie's mouth, and, for a moment, I can't believe it. I've always known she would do anything for me like I would for her, but her serious side isn't one we see very often.

Ella nods and smiles softly. "Kenzie's right. I've been thinking about your situation, and I know I said before that you shouldn't give up all of your hard work for a man, but what if you don't have to? What if you took a chance and just see what happens? It's not like you get this way with every guy who talks to you. Whatever is going on is different and you know it, or you wouldn't be struggling so badly. Do you really want to wonder what might have been if you decide to say no to Colin?"

Damn it. No, I didn't want to wonder, but the frightening feeling of this all going sideways is a lot to overcome.

Kenzie briefly points her camera toward her chest. "I have never wanted to shove your face into my breasts and hold you tighter than I do right now, but since I can't, I'll just say one more thing. We love you, Piper. You are the best part of our friendship. You know what you need to do. You knew the moment he kissed you again in that elevator. Follow that little voice and see where it takes you."

I'm half laughing and half crying by the time she's done, and so is Ella as she says, "Ditto everything the crazy one says. Only this time she's absolutely right, and we both know it."

Ella blows me a kiss and Kenzie does the same before they both hang up. I toss my phone toward the end of the couch and throw my head back.

Am I really going to take the biggest risk I've ever taken in my life? And all for a guy?

Holy hell, I am.

Chapter Twelve

WITH MY TEETH

Colin

THAT MAY NOT HAVE GONE HOW I HOPED IT would, but all things considered, I'm not disappointed with getting everything out there between the two of us.

Sure, I only just met Piper and might have scared the hell out of her with my declarations, but at a certain point in life, when you know, you know. There's no point in trying to deny things when they're smacking me right in the face.

After having said my piece, I spent the rest of the weekend able to relax. There is nothing more I can do, and I won't pursue Piper after this. I don't want to force her into something she could regret later.

Knowing I'd done what I needed to allowed me to focus on other things, like building a bookshelf in my office at home. It had taken me all of Sunday, but at least all of the books I'd paid thousands of dollars to ship overseas now had a proper place in the house.

Now, it's Monday morning and I find myself feeling

ready for the day. There are no more nerves or anxiety inside me.

When I get into my office early, I reply to emails first and check the clock a few times. Nothing has changed here. I still intend to sit with Piper this morning and finish my observation of her integrating the work I know she did at home this weekend back into the piles she had strewn about on her desk Friday.

A few minutes before eight, I get up and grab my notepad. When I turn for the door, I see Brian leaning against the frame.

"Hey, man. I tried to call you this weekend. Thought you might have wanted to go out again with us," he says.

I smile and shrug. "Sorry. I was busy doing stuff around the house, and I don't think I'll be going out again."

Brian cocks his brow. "Found yourself a woman already? Is it that beauty I saw you with on the dance floor at the club?"

Fuck. He'd seen us? Well, maybe not entirely. He'd said "beauty", not Piper. So, it had to be fine.

"Nah. It's just not for me. At least not every weekend. You'll be the first person I call when I feel like letting loose, though," I say and take a step forward, hoping he leaves without me having to tell him I'm busy.

He nods and holds his fist out. "You better, or you'll never hear the end of it from us. The guys all liked you once you relaxed a little."

I bump his fist, since it seems as if he's not going to move until I do. "Thanks." Hopefully that's the proper response. These guys are nothing like the friends I had back home. We didn't do clubs. We had private gatherings that didn't need loud music and sloppy dancing to be fun.

Yes, I realize that makes me sound old, but I enjoyed

myself and met a lot of great people thanks to those parties. I mean, it wasn't like we sat around playing chess.

Once Brian heads back to his office, I make my way to Piper's. Her door is open, and I step inside to find her bent over the desk with her back to me, attempting to organize the papers as I assumed she would be.

"I almost missed the show," I say teasingly, but it isn't until she swirls around with wide eyes that I realize it came out wrong.

That doesn't mean I hadn't also been thinking about what it might be like to take her over this desk and make her scream my name. Though, that's not the thought she's going to want to hear.

I point to the papers. "I was wondering earlier how you were going to organize all of your notes once you came back in."

Her shoulders drop. "Oh. Right. I only have three piles normally, and I need them to be in chapter order for my work later to make sense, so it looks like a disaster now, but it's not."

Moving further into the office, I make sure to give her enough space. "Do you want help?"

She bites her lip and shakes her head. "I'm almost done. Sorry, I didn't think you were coming this morning, or I would have waited."

My eyes meet hers, and I hope they convey the patience I feel inside. "Nothing has changed here, Piper. Whatever was said this weekend has no effect on what happens in the office, as long as we don't let it, and I don't intend to."

She looks down at the desk and takes a deep breath. While she's processing what I've said, I take a moment to appreciate her formfitting black slacks and the red blouse with a small bow just below her neck that I would love to undo with my teeth.

Finally, she meets my gaze again. "You're right. I'm sorry."

I nearly reach for her, then think better of it. "You have nothing to apologize for. Well, maybe you do. May I ask something I didn't before?"

Piper's jaw tightens, and she glances at the door. "Uh, sure."

My finger points to all of the papers. "Why do you print them?"

"Oh." Her mouth forms a circle as the singular word falls from her lips. I don't think she really believes me when I say nothing with work has to change. I'll have to be extra sure to show her that, especially until she makes her decision about us.

"Well, it's easier for me to do a second round of edits when my mind isn't distracted by the comments I've already left. Maybe I was in a mood before and missed something or judged it too harshly. I like to know that my opinions are in the best interest of the author and their book, not clouded by my personal feelings."

That isn't the answer I was expecting, and I feel bad for what I'm about to say, but again, I'm here to make things easier, and I can't hold back when I see something that could be improved.

"What if you just had two electronic files and once you were done, you could merge the documents and all of the comments you left would appear together." My suggestion is simple, yet the shock on her face is anything but.

She blinks several times. "I don't know. That's just how my old editor did things. I picked up her process without thinking much about it, but you're right. That way would save the company money and me possibly hours of time. I don't know why I never thought to do something differently."

My lips curve into a smile, and I reach for her elbow, unable to stop myself from touching her any longer. "That's why we're doing this. It's easy to continue doing the same thing over and over again because it's comfortable...safe. But there's nothing wrong with change when it has good intentions."

Piper glances down where my hand is wrapped around her elbow. When she looks back up at me, there's a softness in her eyes I've yet to see. Like a window to her world that I would love to lose myself in.

"Thank you," she says quietly, then steps away and resumes shuffling papers. "I'll make two electronic copies for the next book I work on and let you know how it goes."

I nod, then wait quietly as she finishes organizing the chapters however works for her current system.

She hasn't given an inkling as to whether or not she's made a decision about my asking her to risk her job to date me, but I didn't expect an answer so soon. Not from this woman. I have a feeling after watching her work and the few conversations we've had that even if she's made up her mind already, she'll wait days, possibly weeks, before she says the words out loud.

It's a trait I equally admire and hate right now.

When she's done, I take my seat. This time, the door stays open, and I keep my chair on the opposite side of the desk from her.

At my suggestion, Piper quickly explains why she's been editing the way she has and how everything works. I listen intently and take more notes, because even though I hope she'll switch to editing all through the electronic copies, that doesn't mean there isn't a piece of her process that could be helpful in other ways.

"So, that's it. I still have fifteen more chapters to get through, and once I combine everything, I skim through notes one more time to make sure I've written them clearly and concisely, then I do my editorial letter and email everything to the author." She lets out a heavy breath and reaches for a bottle of water at the back of her desk.

My eyes watch the way her blouse rises and shows just a sliver of creamy skin at her waist. Damn, I hope she says yes and doesn't make me wait long.

We continue to keep things only business. We chat about books we've worked on, things we love most about our job, and what we hope to accomplish.

I can't stop myself from smiling when I finally exit her office just before lunch. During the couple of hours we spent just talking—of course, keeping it work-related—there wasn't an ounce of awkwardness between us.

After Piper warmed up, I was able to watch the way her eyes glistened when she talked about the things she was truly passionate about, like finding those diamond-in-the-rough stories with authors who just want to learn and use their words to help people escape from reality for a short time.

As passionate as she was about that part of the process, I'm surprised she's not a writer herself, but when I asked if she'd ever written anything, she waved me off and said, "once an editor, always an editor."

I whistle softly as I make my way back to my office and find Steve headed in my direction. For once, I don't dread seeing him.

He reaches a hand toward me, and we shake. "Good day so far?" he asks.

"Absolutely. I just finished up with the first employee I decided to shadow, and I can already see we're going to be able to make positive changes," I say.

His fist nudges my shoulder. "I'm glad to hear it. Let me know if you need anything before Thursday. I'll be gone for a few days, but my assistant Carla will still be around if there's something urgent."

I nod and adjust the papers in my hands. "Hopefully, you're taking holiday somewhere fun?"

Steve grimaces and lowers his voice as his face gets closer to mine. "I wish. The wife is taking me to her sister's fifth wedding. Like we haven't seen her get married enough already."

My shoulders shake with laughter as he walks past me. "Good luck with that," I call before heading into my office.

As I sit down in my chair and put my notes on the desk, I lean back and grin. Maybe moving all the way to the U.S. for a job wasn't the craziest idea I've ever had.

Piper is perfect in every way, and I just hope she allows me to show her that I could be the same for her.

Chapter Thirteen

BLOODY HELL

Piper

NEARLY THREE ACHINGLY LONG, YET INTERESTING weeks have passed since Colin was in my kitchen and asked me to take a risk with him. I'd decided that day that I wanted to give things a try with him and let future Piper deal with the fallout, but I'd wanted time to get to know Colin without the complication of feelings between us. To experience how work could be if we didn't make things messy.

I'm not sure if seeing how easy everything has felt between us makes my decision harder or easier, but either way, I haven't changed my mind about seeing what happens.

I spent quite a bit of time with Colin. A part of me was testing him, and I felt only slightly bad about that. Not once did he ask me if I'd made up my mind. Not once did he try to kiss me or touch me in any way that was romantic. We were merely coworkers getting to know each other as friends.

If that didn't punch me right in all the feels, I didn't know what would.

I'd finally had enough of this arms-length, friendship thing we were doing. Ever since our last kiss at my house, I haven't forgotten the press of his lips against mine, the feel of his hard length, or the gentle way he held me.

It's Friday night, and I stayed late at work so that I don't have to bring anything home with me for the weekend. I intend to pay Colin a surprise visit at his house. I found out where he lives when I saw his car parked in the driveway on my way home last week. When he'd been jogging around my house, I didn't consider he might live only a few blocks away.

Apparently, the universe isn't done pushing us together.

Telling him I'm ready to try isn't easy, but I know I can't be left wondering what might have been. I need to know if this man could be worth whatever might happen in the future.

Yes, I love my job, but I've only made work such a priority because it's safe. Work can't hurt me as long as I do my job to the best of my ability.

I'm not getting any younger, and seeing my two best friends fall in love...well, it's made me reevaluate some things.

After logging off my computer and grabbing my purse, I flick the lights off and head for the elevator.

While I'm waiting for the doors to open, I search for my phone and can't find it. I turn around to go check my desk, but a glow of light coming from another office distracts me. Tiptoeing forward, I stay quiet and peek to see who's still here with me because they've been quiet as a mouse. Also, maybe because I secretly hope I know who's still here.

I see the door to Colin's office is closed, and an idea immediately starts to form in my mind. Something spontaneous and not me, but I don't want to be afraid to act on my first thoughts anymore.

When I get back to my office, I grab my phone and dim the light on the screen since I'm in the dark room. Thank you, Shannon, for sharing everyone's numbers with me for those just-in-case situations I didn't think I'd ever have.

Me: *What are you doing right now?*

I've never contacted Colin, so he shouldn't know this is me, and I hope to screw with him a bit before popping into his office.

Colin: *Working late. You?*

Not the answer I expected, but I can work with this.

Me: *Wondering why a guy like you would be working so late on a Friday...alone.*

I hear a snort-laugh from down the hall.

Colin: *Because the girl I want isn't ready for me. At least I didn't think so...*

What the hell does that mean? This is not working out how I wanted.

Me: *Well, I'm sure it's her loss.*

Colin: *What are you saying, Piper?*

I gasp, and my phone clatters onto my metal desk. How the hell does he know it's me? Shit. Why didn't I realize that if Shannon has everyone's number that the others probably do as well?

I feel like such an idiot.

"Piper?" Colin calls from the hallway.

Instead of stepping out to meet him, I transform into a crazy person and decide to hide under my desk in hopes he'll just go back to his office when he can't see anything.

After all my attempts to banter with Kenzie, I should

have known I couldn't pull off screwing with Colin over text.

His footfalls sound closer, and I stop breathing, afraid to make even the slightest noise. I'm just grateful my light was already off.

Then, my mother-freaking phone starts to vibrate. On the metal desktop.

The light turns on. My face heats. I'm frozen in the ball I've attempted to form into under my desk.

Colin walks around the desk and bends down, settling onto a knee. He smiles, and there's a tightness in his face that tells me he's doing everything he can not to laugh his ass off right now.

"What are you doing down there?" he asks casually with a raised brow, looking around me for a second before meeting my flaming face again.

"Dropped something. Couldn't find it. I'm done now, though." My fingers uncurl from my knees, and I put my palms on the floor to get up, but I'm still too far under the desk and don't realize it.

My head slams into the underside of the desk, and I see stars.

Blinking rapidly, I'm back on my ass and wobbling to the side, but Colin catches me before I can fall over.

"Whoa, let me help you." His hands reach for my ribs, pulling me toward him, and this is the closest we've been since the night at my house.

Heat leaves my face and travels south, especially when I realize I'm wearing a dress today and might have been showing him more than he bargained for when he first walked in.

Slowly, Colin helps me stand, but my knees are shaking

with weeks of pent-up sexual tension. I don't know that I can be alone with him right now. I didn't expect to see him so soon. I shouldn't have texted him. I should have just gone the hell home like I'd intended and waited to show up at his house.

He peers into my eyes, then without saying anything, shines the light from his phone into my face.

I swat his hand away and turn my head to the side. "What the hell was that for?"

He chuckles and puts his phone in his pocket. "Just checking to see if you had a concussion. Probably not but can't be too careful." Then, he nods at my desk where my traitorous phone still is. "So, what was going on with those texts?"

My head shakes and thankfully the action isn't painful. The only thing I'd truly hurt was my pride. "They were nothing. Call it a moment of insanity when I thought you didn't have my number."

His smile grows, and he leans closer to me. "Work phone tree, as Sandy called it. She passed them out earlier this week. Maybe you missed it, but if so, I should be asking how you have mine, Ms. Fitz."

Cheese and freaking rice. Why does everything I say to this man seem to backfire on me?

His nearness is invading my every sense, and I'm thankful my ass is resting on the desk. My eyes roam over his face, then down his chest where I see he's ditched his tie and suit coat for the evening. He's only wearing a soft-blue shirt that brings out his eyes and black slacks with the most perfect creases over his legs.

When I make my way back to his face, he's still staring at me, but his face is much closer than before my perusal.

"Piper, you can't look at me like that and expect me to

keep my hands to myself for very long. Should I go?" he asks, his words sounding almost painful.

My head shakes ever so slightly. "Don't go. I want you to stay. Right here."

"Thank fuck," he murmurs, then our mouths crash together in a symphony of heated tension. Lips, teeth, tongues. I don't know whose is whose. All I do know is that Colin's hands are roaming over my body. I have one wrapped around the back of his neck, making sure he doesn't pull away from me. My fingers of the other hand are clutching the front of his shirt as I do my best not to look like a sex-crazed fiend.

His mouth travels down to my neck. "Are you sure about this?"

I push him back so that he can see the seriousness in my face. "I've spent the last three weeks making sure I was. If I say I am, you don't need to question me. Not now, not ever."

"So perfect," he mutters as I bring him back to me.

My back arches, and I push forward, but he picks me up and sits my ass firmly on the desk. My dress billows around me, and I wince from the unexpected coolness of the surface on my ass.

His palms brand themselves into my thighs as he grips them tightly and presses his forehead against mine.

"I know you're sure, but I haven't forgotten that we're at work right now. How *sure* are you?" he asks, and his hands move dangerously far up my legs.

My skin shivers, and my core tightens with anticipation. The ride home is going to be painful if I don't let him take the edge off, and right now, work is the last thing I'm worried about. The fact that he cares enough to ask only makes me want him more. Right this very moment.

"Sure enough to let you touch me," I finally say and scoot forward on the desk.

"Bloody hell," he mutters, then kisses me with a frenzy I've yet to see from him. I'm so distracted by what the swirling of his tongue is doing to my insides, that I don't register his hand has made its way up until my underwear has already been pushed to the side and his finger trails lightly over my slit.

Bloody hell is right. I'm practically clawing at his shoulders to encourage him. I suddenly can't stand the thought of not having his touch on me right fucking now. My breathing is ragged, and everything inside me aches.

Clearly, I haven't been taking as good of care of my body as I should have been lately.

Colin drags me forward until I'm barely on the desk and my legs are spread wide open for him. Once I'm right where he wants me, he slips a finger inside me, and I grip his biceps until my knuckles turn white.

He pumps his hand once, then twice, and I'm already squeezing hard around his finger. Then, his thumb presses against my clit, and I see spots in my vision.

My head drops forward against his chest, and I focus on calming my neediness. I can't come when he's only just gotten started. Not when I know what will happen next.

"So fucking tight," he whispers against my ear. "And your scent... I thought it was driving me wild before."

His hand moves faster, and he adds another finger to the titillating movements. Between his words and actions, I'm not sure how much longer I can hold on.

"This is only the appetizer, Piper. Don't fight your own release."

His command is like a punch to my detonate button. I tighten my legs around his waist, and my head presses further into his chest. My spine stiffens and legs ache, but the euphoria that rolls through me in the seconds after the buildup...that is everything I haven't been able to give myself since my last proper date.

I shudder and tremble and moan—possibly a little too loudly—and I ride Colin's hand shamelessly as the waves rocking my body slow. Only then do my muscles uncoil, and I release the death grip I've had on him this whole time.

His hand slowly pulls out from between my legs, and he reaches for a tissue from the box beside my monitor.

He hands me one, but I scrunch my nose. "That is going nowhere near my vagina. Tissues aren't meant to be toilet paper." Colin's already wiping his hand off, and I point to the ripped pieces. "See? None of that nonsense is going where it doesn't belong."

Surprising the hell out of me, he leans forward and captures my mouth for a quick yet powerful kiss. "I'll get you something more suitable then, so we can get out of here."

Shivers race down my arms when he says "we". I assumed we'd both go our separate ways once we left the office, but I'm not opposed to spending the rest of the evening together. Not after that little performance on my desk.

Shit, I just may *need* this night with him if I expect to get any decent sleep.

Chapter Fourteen

Colin

I'VE NEVER BEEN MORE GRATEFUL TO BE A workaholic than I am right now. My grin stretches wide across my face as I head to get Piper some paper towels from the loo down the hall.

When she texted me, I was so confused. I thought she was saying yes to my proposal in a really weird way, then it seemed more like a no.

Though, her having no idea I had her number and finding her hiding under the desk... That was perfect.

I enter the washroom and turn the faucet on warm before pulling a few paper towels from the holder. Since I'm already there, I quickly wash my hands and then finish up.

When I walk back to her office, I'm still picturing Piper wrapped around me and coming undone in a matter of minutes all because of my fingers. My cock is harder than it's ever been, and the need to take her again on the desk is strong, but I don't want all of our firsts to be in this office or work-related.

She deserves better. I'm going to show her how true that is just as soon as we're behind proper closed doors.

I walk into her office to find her still perched on the desk and red in the face. "This is really awkward."

I wink at her and hand over the paper towels. "Only if you let it be. For me, this is everything."

The blush on her cheeks deepens, and I brush strands of her silky hair back when she tries to hide behind them.

"Don't overthink this. We're just two adults who are attracted to each other and seeing where that attraction leads before we make any big decisions. Ones that we don't need to think about now, because neither of us can tell the future."

That last bit is near painful for me to say, but I don't want Piper to overthink anything. Sure, I want her to make decisions for herself and not because I want them, but what I feel isn't one-sided, either. There are real feelings between us, and I don't want fear to be the thing that keeps us from knowing what might have been.

Piper uses one paper towel to wipe her desk off and then the remaining to clean herself. She says nothing as she does, and my nerves run rampant.

I'm tempted to keep rambling, but I don't think that would help anything, so I patiently wait for her to be ready to talk just like I have these last few weeks.

Sure, I've wanked off in the shower more than usual, but the wait has been worth it, and I know if Piper still isn't ready, then I'll gladly continue to be patient.

She throws the towels away and chuckles. "At least the trash will get taken out tomorrow by the cleaners."

I'm not sure what thoughts were running through her head before that, but I merely nod and smile in response, still waiting for her to tell me what she wants.

Her teeth scrape her bottom lip, and she looks left then right before finally meeting my gaze. "I don't do this. Hell, I haven't even really dated in years."

No wonder she was fucking tight when I touched her.

She runs a hand through her hair and sighs. "I want to go home with you, and I know what will happen if I do. Before you say that we don't have to have sex, we most certainly do. Especially after that little performance." Her gaze cuts toward the desk. "I just need you to know whatever this is, I might not handle everything well all the time. I'm the rational one out of my friends. I don't do crazy shit like they do. Though, sometimes I do encourage their idiocy and I've seen that work out for them. Even more so lately. So, before I continue to ramble and make an even bigger fool of myself and you decide that being with me is a bad idea, I'm going to say this once and then we're going to leave. I want to go home with you, Colin. I want to have sex with you tonight. But most of all, I want to trust you when you say this won't all backfire on both of us."

My feet move of their own accord, and by the time she's done speaking, I'm standing only inches away from her. I raise my hands and cup her face. "Thank you for trusting me. Nothing you've said could possibly change my mind about you. Whatever happens, I'll still be here and do whatever I can to keep you safe from any potential fallout. I promise." I kiss her forehead, then hold out one of my hands. "Are you ready to get out of here?"

She glances toward the hallway. "Are you sure there aren't cameras in this building? Shannon said there weren't, but maybe management doesn't want the employees to know they're being watched."

"There are no cameras to my knowledge, and I think they would have said something by now, especially when the great lunch debacle happened on the second floor." I shake my head just remembering all the yelling while I was working down there.

Piper finally takes my offered hand and grabs her bag with the other before we go to my office to get my things. When we get back in the hallway, she finally asks, "What happened with the lunches?"

I laugh nervously since the strong change of subject doesn't seem like the best idea, but I go with it anyway. "Sally from accounting had just paid for some expensive food subscription box and was bringing the meals to work for lunch and snacks. Half of them went in the fridge, but with the overcrowding of employees, people's food didn't always fare well. Sally's, especially. Her stuff started to go missing, and she sent a polite email about it, then more days passed with more lunches taken and every email got progressively more hostile until she finally stood on her desk and yelled at every single person who could hear."

Piper's mouth popped open in shock. "Did she get fired or find out who was taking her food?"

"Nope, neither of those things happened. Steve sent his own email out that if we couldn't be adults and not respect other people's belongings that he would have to put cameras up. Sally's lunches have been safe ever since, as far as I know."

It really was one of the highlights during my time spent sitting with the different departments while I waited for mine to be ready.

I release Piper's hand to log off my computer and grab my things. Her shoulders are still shaking with laughter when I'm ready to go.

"I kind of wish I'd been here to see that, but one of my best friends got married last month, so I'm also glad my move date got pushed out as far as it did," Piper says, and a longing pulls her expression down.

My hand captures hers again, and I lead us to the lift. "I saw the picture on your desk when I was taking notes about your process. Was it hard to leave them?"

She frowns and adjusts the hold on her bag as we walk. "Probably one of the hardest things I've ever done. Ella, Kenzie, and I have been best friends since grade school. I've experienced every big moment of my life with them. Taking this job and knowing that now we won't all be together for those moments... It's rather devastating, actually."

My chest aches for her. I had friends back home, but nobody who would have made me think twice about starting this new adventure in the US.

"I'm sure they tried to talk you out of coming," I say as we step onto the lift.

Her head shakes, and she presses the button for the parking garage first. "Not once. Well, Kenzie might have joked and been partially serious, but they were both really supportive. They're going to fly out here soon to see everything in person."

I give her hand another squeeze. "Maybe I can meet them while they're here."

She doesn't say anything the rest of the ride down and when we head for our cars that aren't parked too far from each other, her smile doesn't quite reach her face any longer.

"Do you want to drive together or follow me?" I ask with as much confidence as I can muster, hoping like hell she hasn't changed her mind thanks to my presumptuous comment.

"I'll follow you. Probably wouldn't look good for my car to be here when I'm not, in case anyone else comes in or when security does their rounds," she replies with a bit of a smirk. I let my shoulders relax some.

With a quick nod, I unlock my car. "I'll see you shortly, then."

I wait to get all the way in my car until she's already buckling up inside hers. My briefcase gets tossed in the passenger's seat, and I desperately try to remember if I left anything out like dirty trousers that I'll need to race inside the house to clean up first.

I hadn't expected Piper to make her decision so soon. Once a few days had passed and she hadn't said anything, I thought there might be months of proving I could be professional with her at work before she agreed to date me in secret.

This night is turning out to be even better than I could have predicted.

Thankfully, our neighborhood isn't far from the office, and within twenty minutes, we're turning onto my road. I can see Sir Charles in the window, and his head pops up when I click the garage opener.

He's going to be a mouthy bastard since he's getting his supper late, but hopefully the canned food I've been saving for a special occasion will appease him and allow me some time alone with Piper before he begins meowing all over the house.

When I get out of my car, I leave the garage door open and point out my window for Piper to park next to me. I don't want her to worry about anyone seeing her car at my house, and I didn't bring much stuff with me from London, so there's plenty of room inside the garage.

She gets out of her car and smiles. "Good idea parking in here."

"I figured that would help quell some of your unease," I

say, waiting for her to join me at the front of my car before I lead us inside.

As soon as I get the door unlocked and open, the freaking cat pounces at my ankles and lets out a screeching meow.

"Bloody hell, cat. Calm down. I'll feed you as soon as I set my stuff down," I say and gently nudge him away so we can get in the door.

Piper bends down and calls for him. "Come here, sweet baby." She looks up at me. "Where's his food?"

"Oh, you don't have to do that," I say, but both Piper and the cat narrow their eyes at me. "In the cabinet right there."

Piper follows the direction of my finger and starts talking to my cat in an adorable baby voice. "We'll get your belly full. Yes, we will. Don't you worry about a thing." Then, she turns back to me. "I'm assuming his name isn't cat?"

I grimace. "It's Sir Charles, but I call him Charlie most of the time. He was my mother's before she passed, and I didn't have the heart to leave him behind when I moved."

Her smile brightens. "You're a good man, Colin." She goes back to giving the cat all of her attention and I use that time to do a quick run-through of the house.

All the while, I think I finally like the cat a little more now.

Chapter Fifteen

OVERLY EAGER LIBIDO

Piper

NERVES HAD COMPLETELY DESTROYED ME ON THE drive over. I had no idea what I was doing following this sexy man to his house, knowing damn well what was going to happen.

This isn't me. I don't do things without thinking them through until every piece of the scenario has been analyzed.

Except, I'd already done that, which is why I made the conscious decision to ask Colin to take me home. Still, I find myself back in my own head after that epic orgasm on my desk and the way he offered to get me paper towels to clean myself up.

Colin is respectful, but there's an underlying power I feel simmering inside him. The man knows what he wants, and he has the patience to wait for something he deems worth waiting for. Knowing I'm something he finds worthy...that does a whole lot to my insides.

Thankfully, when we walked inside his house, my mood immediately changed upon seeing his cat. I'd always wanted a cat growing up, but my mother is allergic. Seeing his waiting there all fluffy and perfect, I couldn't help but forget about all my worries.

"You're such a handsome boy, Sir Charles, aren't you?" I sweet talk the silky, gray long-haired cat, and he purrs on demand for me while he eats the food I put into a bowl for him.

Colin's arms wrap around my waist, and he rests his chin on my shoulder. "You knew about my cat ahead of time, didn't you? That's the real reason you agreed to come over. I know it."

His tone is joking, but I keep my face neutral. "Maybe. I have a soft spot for kitties."

One of his hands moves slowly over my stomach. "So do I."

Mother shit.

My knees shake, and I lean further into him while his fingers bunch up the ends of my dress. "Would you like to see the rest of the house, starting with the bedroom?"

Oh, God. This is it. If I say yes, there's no turning back. I'll have gone all in. I'll be breaking a condition to the contract I signed with my work. I'll be putting everything on the line. For him.

I can hear Kenzie and Ella in my head, their encouragement to take the risk, to not have any regrets of wondering what may have been, to allow myself to do something selfish.

Turning around in Colin's arms, I wrap my hands around his neck and grin. "The bedroom sounds like a wonderful place to start."

He grips my hips and lifts me off the ground. My legs wrap around his waist, and I lean forward to kiss him when he starts walking.

We turn a corner too sharply, and his shoulder slams into the wall, causing me to laugh at his expense. "Oops," I say since I was the one who initiated the kiss.

"Worth any bruises that might appear later," he says, voice deeper than normal. His pace quickens, and I don't really get to look around the house, but I catch there's a small dining area outside the kitchen, a living room to the right of that, and then a hallway with several doors, most of which are closed.

He stops at the last one and shoves it open. Instead of letting me back down to stand, Colin carries me to the bed, then drops me onto his mattress.

Okay, there's not even going to be a small semblance of a tour before continuing what we started at work.

I thought that might bother me, but this is probably better considering I have a tendency to overthink things. Now is definitely not the time to be doing that.

Colin's hands grip my thighs lightly, then trail down until he's gripping my ankles. My skin prickles with heightened energy and he props one of my feet against his chest while he begins undoing the strap to my heel.

"As part of the tour, I should go over the rules for the house," he says, leaning forward to kiss the top of my foot. "The first is there are no shoes allowed in the bed."

I lick my lips and smirk. "A great rule. Thank you for stopping me from breaking the top one. What else?"

He tosses the first heel onto an oversized olive-green armchair behind him that I hadn't yet noticed. "The second rule is that there are no expectations of what's going to happen here. We can go tour the living room, put a movie on, and I'd be happy with that."

The fact that I know his words are sincere is exactly why

I have no intentions of leaving this bedroom until we've both had epic orgasms.

I need this more than I think he realizes.

For too long, I've stayed closed off and hidden from everyone except Kenzie and Ella. I took my job and moved across the United States for many reasons, but forcing myself out of my comfort zone is one of the biggest.

"That's good to know, but I don't think I've seen enough of this bedroom yet," I say as he finishes taking off my other shoe, then I reach my hands for him.

He takes a step forward and ends up between my legs. My fingers deftly work at the buttons of his dress shirt. "I don't want you to think I'm here for any other reason than I want to be. You've given me enough time and enough outs. I don't need any more. Okay?"

Colin leans closer and embraces my face with his hands. "Okay." Then, his lips are on mine, and I lose hold of the button I'd been working on.

My ankles wrap around the back of his knees, and I grip his hips while he brands my mouth with his tongue and a tangy taste, like he's recently chewed fruity gum.

He pulls back enough to reach over his shoulder and yank his dress shirt off in one go. "Undoing all those buttons takes too much time."

I grin and tilt my head. "And I know how much you hate wasting time."

His chest rumbles, and his hands are back on my thighs, but this time they move up instead of down. As he gathers the cotton fabric into his hands, his thumbs brush over my simple black underwear and a shudder ripples through me.

"Already needy for more," he says with a hum of approval.

I was "needy for more" the moment he walked out of my office, but I don't tell him that.

My dress comes off next, and I reach for the top of his pants, pulling on the leather belt. "You're suddenly wearing too many clothes."

While he unclasps the belt, I pull down on the zipper and feel his hard cock already trying to bust through the material.

Shit. I'm not sure I can handle *all* of that.

But there's no backing out now. Even if I might feel the ramifications of my choice for the rest of the weekend, I know it will be worth what's about to happen.

Colin shoves his pants down, and he's left in only black boxer briefs. My eyes are growing wider by the second, unable to leave his dick.

He lifts my chin with one hand. "You still with me?"

I nod and lick my suddenly dry lips. "Yep. Right here."

His eyes narrow, but he doesn't say anything else, for which I'm thankful. Instead, he begins to push me back, and I crawl further onto the mattress. The charcoal-colored comforter is thick and filled with feathers, making my hands sink into the soft material.

Colin crawls over me and brushes my hair back against his pillow. I expect him to say something more, but words don't leave his mouth. He kisses my forehead, then cheeks, and keeps going, working his way down to my chest.

His hand slides under my back and unclips my bra while his tongue drags slowly over the curve of my breasts. When the bra disappears behind him, he pulls a taut nipple into his mouth, allowing his teeth to scrape lightly over the pebbled skin.

My fingers dig into the comforter as I try to rein in my

overly eager libido. I thought it was the guy who was supposed to feel like a teenager during sex, not the woman.

As he continues devouring my breasts, one of his hands slips between us and begins to slide my underwear down. I lean up to help, and the fabric only makes it to my knees before he has two fingers inside me again.

They curl up expertly, and my pussy contracts around him in time with his movements. My head falls further into the pillows. I'm on sensory overload between his mouth on my chest and fingers fucking me into another orgasm that feels much too soon.

I manage to hold back my release by focusing on Colin. My hands reach for his cock, and my fingers slip under the waistband of his briefs. His silky and wet head is right there, ready to break free from its restraints.

My hand wraps around the pulsing dick, and I squeeze while simultaneously pushing and pulling. He feels even bigger in my grip, but I try not to focus on the size. Instead, I lose myself in the rapid beat of my heart, the tingling over my skin that is racing through my body, and the tightening of my core as Colin continues to ravish the upper half of my body with his mouth.

The faint glow from Colin's alarm clock shines around us now that my eyes have adjusted to the dark, allowing me to see his smiling face when he pulls up, resting on his knees that are on both sides of my hips. "Don't move," he says before getting off the bed.

I see him ditch his boxers as he heads to what I assume is the bathroom, and I kick my underwear the rest of the way off. By the time he returns, I'm propped up on my elbows and attempting to tame my hair from where his hands have tangled the long strands.

Colin holds up a pack of condoms, and I'm grateful he

thought of that, because it honestly hadn't even crossed my mind. I've at least kept up on my birth control even though I haven't been having sex, so we'll be doubly safe.

My eyes watch him rip a condom from the pack and tear the plastic open with his teeth. I shudder when I remember how those same teeth felt on my nipples and as they lightly scraped against my sensitive skin.

Colin leans forward and captures my mouth with his while he puts the condom on. "You're fucking beautiful with your flushed cheeks and trembling legs right now," he whispers against my lips. "Even sexier than when I had you coming on top of your desk."

Holy hell. How am I supposed to respond to that? I've never talked much during sex before, so this is all new territory for me.

He doesn't wait for me to respond—at least, not with words—before he's getting back up on the bed and settling himself over me.

I reach for his biceps as I lower myself back onto the pillows behind me. Colin's eyes never leave mine while he reaches between us, teases my clit with the thick head of his cock, and then begins to push inside me.

Shit. He's even bigger than I realized, or I'm tighter than I expected. Either way, this isn't an easy fit.

Colin keeps even pressure, moving forward gently. Thankfully, I'm wet enough that there's no other resistance besides the repercussions of my unused pussy.

God, this is so embarrassing.

My eyes close when he's only halfway in. While it feels good and he's not hurting me, I can imagine this is weird for him.

His thumb strokes my cheek, and his lips gently glide over mine as he pauses. "Piper, look at me."

With only slight hesitation, I do as he asks.

"Are you...a, um, virgin?" he asks quietly and with a bit of a frown on his face.

Heat from embarrassment licks at my skin, making my chest and cheeks feel like they're on fire. "No. Absolutely not."

His eyes soften, and he offers me a small smile. "There's nothing to be embarrassed about. I just wanted to be sure."

I throw an arm over my face. "What if you don't fit?"

His chuckle echoes through the otherwise quiet room. "Oh, I'm going to fit and you're going to enjoy every inch."

Those words only have my pussy tightening all over again, and he shakes his head. "But you're going to have to relax for that to happen."

With a slight nod, I do my best to not focus on the size of his massive cock, but instead on the fact that Colin is showing me even more of his patience and kindness and how fucking sexy I find the way he treats me.

My legs spread as wide as they'll go, and he's still not all the way seated inside me. He reaches behind my head and shoves the pillows aside so that I'm lying flat. Once I am, his left hand moves to my lower back and lifts until my hips tilt and my ass is in the air. Then, he reaches for one of the discarded pillows and slides it underneath me.

Before I can adjust to the new position, he pulls back and slams forward. The action steals my breath, and my nails dig into his arms.

"Holy shit. Do that again," I pant, grinding against him.

He smirks and leans down until our noses are touching. "That last bit had to be forced in. Glad I didn't hurt you, but we're still going to keep the pounding to a minimum or you'll hate me tomorrow."

I contract around him when he says "pounding" with his British inflection. I've never in my life been more attracted to an accent than I am right fucking now.

Colin resumes his gentle movements and, given my recent lack of experience, all I can do is hold on for the ride. And what a glorious one it is.

His hips move rhythmically, and his dick fills me deeper than even my gynecologist has been.

"I'm already so close," I murmur against his lips.

"Don't worry. So am I." His face is filled with tension, and I can see veins bulging along his neck. "Between your tight pussy and the weeks I've spent dreaming about this, you'll have to forgive the quickness."

Shivers rock my entire body, and he grunts above me, pressing his forehead to mine and sliding a hand between us.

His thumb rubs over my clit, and I can't hold in my gasp at the pleasure that blasts through me when he does.

Spots fill my vision from squeezing my eyes so hard, and I tilt my head back onto the mattress. Colin's movements slow above me, and his breathing is ragged when I feel his weight settle onto me as he moves to rest on his elbows.

When I reopen my eyes and look up at him, he's grinning and playing with the ends of my hair with one hand. "That was so much more than I imagined it would be."

I raise a brow. "How often have you imagined this?"

His eyes darken, and the smile falls from his face. "More times than I should tell you."

Hell, this man is going to destroy me, body and soul. I already know it. Yet, there isn't any part of me that wants to do anything to stop that from happening.

Chapter Sixteen

LESS ENDOWED

Colin

MY THOUGHTS ARE A JUMBLED MESS AS I HEAD TO the toilet to dispose of the condom and get Piper a warm washcloth. I knew she was going to be different from any other woman I'd been with, but I hadn't expected her to be so tight and responsive.

A much larger part of me wanted to ravage her, but when I couldn't get my cock to go right in her tight pussy, I knew I would need to be gentle with her. At least, for now. Which is probably better. With my luck, I'd have scared her away with my adventurous nature in bed.

When I get back into the bedroom, Piper has the pillows back behind her head and her legs are crossed, likely trying to keep all those wonderful juices of hers from leaking onto the duvet.

Testing the waters, since she seems to be rather shy about sex, I pull her ankles until her ass is at the edge of the bed. I purposely left the restroom light on so I can see her swollen lips with my own eyes.

She tenses when I bend to my knees and start to spread her legs apart. "Colin..."

"I'm just cleaning up my mess, love." As soon as the last word leaves my mouth, I slowly glance up at Piper to find her eyes wide. "Term of endearment where I'm from," I add with a crooked grin.

She lets out a moderate breath, and I go back to relishing in her perfection. Gently, I lay the washcloth over her sweet center and drag the soft material down until I hit the bed, then I fold that corner and start over again, but this time from the bottom of her ass cheeks.

Piper's intake of air doesn't surprise me, but I keep going since she hasn't asked me to stop. Next, I clean up her inner thighs. By the time I'm done, she's trembling all over again, and her chest is heaving when I stand.

The back of my hand grazes her cheek. "Soon. I promise, you don't want to go again. Not when it's been so long for you."

She could have been with men less endowed than me, but I'd rather not think too much about that.

Piper nods and nibbles nervously at her lip. "Pretty sure it's been over two years. I focused a lot on work for probably much too long."

I step between her legs, forgetting I'm still naked and already getting hard again until her eyes flick down to my cock. I raise her chin and wait to speak until her eyes meet mine. "Don't feel guilty about putting work ahead of anything else. If that's what you wanted most, then I'm glad you didn't let anyone distract you from that."

She finally grins. "Until now."

I press my lips to hers quickly. "And for that, I'm immensely grateful."

Deciding I should cover my growing erection before she

convinces me to fuck her again, I step away and head to my dresser. Black sweatpants are the first thing I see in the drawer, so I put those on before turning around.

Piper already has her bra back on, and she's wiggling into her underwear when I ask, "Do you want me to grab one of my shirts or are you ready to head home?"

"My dress is pretty comfortable, so I can wear that, and we can watch that movie you mentioned earlier if you want," she says, voice a little shaky.

A knot loosens in my chest as I smile. "Absolutely."

I don't know how I would have felt if she wanted to leave so soon. Actually, that's a lie. I do know. I would have been utterly gutted.

My steps take me straight toward her, and I kiss her again because I can't help myself. "I'll go find something to watch while you finish getting dressed. Feel free to use my bathroom for whatever else you need before you come out."

She nods and offers me a smile before I turn to leave the room. I fight glancing back when I get to the door and force my feet to take me forward.

Charlie is sound asleep on the middle couch cushion when I reach the living room. I consider kicking him off but think better of it.

Piper was so excited earlier when she saw him, she might want to snuggle with the furball. I sit next to him and reach for the remote, clicking the button for a streaming service that should have something funny we can watch.

I head to the movie sections and hear the toilet flush. Good. She's making herself at home. That's what I hoped for when I left her alone.

Unsure what Piper might want to watch, I select something from the top ten watched list and hope for the best.

Another few minutes pass before she treads quietly down my hallway, glancing at the photos on the wall. There aren't many of them, but I did put up a few of my parents, my brother who is living in Scotland now, and a few photos from hiking trips I've taken with scenery that took my breath away.

Just as I assumed would happen, when Piper spots Charlie, a huge smile spreads across her face. "Can I pick him up?" she asks.

"Go for it. He'll love the attention. Not that I deprive him of much. He sleeps in my bed like the king he believes he is," I joke.

Piper picks him up, and I can already hear the purrs coming from the spoiled beast. His head presses against her face, and she giggles. "Well, hello again, sweet boy. Do you want to watch the movie with us?"

He makes a quiet meow, and I think Piper falls in love with the furball right then and there. She finally sits and the cat looks over at me. I swear he smirks while he circles in her lap, claiming *his* spot.

Fucking cat.

As Piper pets Charlie, she looks up at me and she's biting her cheek. "I know it's late, and after what we just did...this probably isn't the best time, but I don't want to stew on this for long."

My hand reaches for her arm, and I gently squeeze. "Having sex doesn't mean we have to pretend everything is going to be sunshine and roses, Piper. Please, don't be afraid to speak your piece with me."

She grins and shakes her head. "I don't understand how you're so patient and kind about all of my hesitancy. I feel like all this...well, mostly me, is going to be too much for you."

I turn until I'm facing her and grasp both of her shoulders. "Not to ruin the moment, but I feel like you need to understand where I'm at with this a little better. I've had long relationships and I've had short ones. I'm thirty-seven years old. After everything I've been through, I've learned to listen to my gut and my heart. They're both demanding me to do whatever it takes to find a way for this to work."

She blinks a few times but stays quiet, so I continue, "There is nothing about you that could be 'too much' for me. Not now and not later, should things progress. I won't hurt you, and I already care a lot about you after getting to know you over the last several weeks." I chuckle, hoping to ease the seriousness I've brought out, then add, "Clearly, I have no problem expressing my feelings, but I'm still okay with giving you all the time you need to feel the same way I do. Tonight doesn't have to change anything, but I'd be more than okay if it does."

Piper takes a few breaths and looks down at the already sleeping cat before meeting my gaze again. "My nervousness doesn't mean I don't feel the same way. It's just harder for me, but I'm ready for things to change. With us. Well, not at work obviously, but otherwise, yes. If you're okay with keeping things quiet between us, then I don't need any more time to think."

I lean forward and press my lips to her forehead. "As long as our secret dating includes exclusivity, nothing would make me happier."

"Of course, there would be exclusivity." Her voice is filled with shock and possibly a little disgust, but I don't apologize for being clear about the ground rules for this "secret dating." Sharing my woman isn't something I could ever handle.

I kiss her again before settling back into the couch cushions. "Good. So, we're under agreement that nothing changes at work. We tell none of our coworkers about each other, and we won't see other people."

I want to add "ever again" at the end of that sentence, but it might be a bit too much for her.

"And no dates outside of the house. We can't go to the local theater or restaurants and risk being seen by anyone who knows us," she says, which is something I hadn't thought about.

While inconvenient and a bit of a disappointment, it's not even close to being a dealbreaker for me. "Why, Ms. Fitz, I think we have a deal."

Her cheeks turn a sexy shade of red, and she nods. "I believe we do as well, Mr. Adamson. Now, how about that movie before I get too sleepy to drive the incredibly long three blocks back to my condo."

My chest tightens. I'd rather have her sleep in my bed tonight, but again, I don't want to push her for too much too fast, so I smile instead and press play on the remote.

Her head leans against my side, and I wrap an arm behind her shoulders before kicking my feet up onto the coffee table.

Damn. It's scary how much I already wish this was all officially mine to have every night and every day for...well, ever.

Chapter Seventeen

EXTRA RUBBER

Piper

COLIN HAD BEEN RIGHT. BY THE TIME I'D HEADED home that night, I was walking bow-legged. It even hurt to pee before I'd gone to bed, but every ache had been more than worth it.

I hadn't realized how much I'd missed having sex until now. At some point, I'd thought Kenzie and Piper were merely exaggerating on the pleasure they got from the action, but nope. It was me who had been missing out. Me who had been failing to live life to the fullest until now.

The rest of the weekend I spent holed up at my house by myself since it was raining. Plus, I wasn't really capable of walking like a normal person until mid-Sunday. Colin had offered to come by, but I'd said no.

Not because I didn't want to see him, but because I really did. Maybe that's weird, but the last thing I need to do is fall hard and fast for this guy, and then what? Quit my job? Have him quit his? Someone gets transferred? Even though I know those are only options at this point, I'm not ready to fully accept them. One of us will end up resenting the other, and that isn't okay with me.

With that realization, it would seem there is no point in trying to continue things, but even my overanalyzing brain can't convince me that is the right solution. I just need things to stay slow for a bit.

I did, at least, work on my book. It's a secret project I've never told anyone about, including my two best friends. I thought I would keep it secret until my dying breath, but since it's now on my list of resolutions, I've been thinking more about what it would feel like to finally finish a first draft and celebrate the massive accomplishment.

For so long, writing has been a passion of mine that helps pass the time when I have nothing else to do. There's something different about this recent book, though, that has me craving to see what transpires on the page next.

I've been trying to contribute the new urges to the craziness that's been happening since the move, but the longer this new drive to finish the book lasts, the more I wonder if it's not time I finally get a little more serious about my passion project.

Except, when I think about anyone else reading the words I let flow from my fingertips—words that are sometimes more of an expression of my inner self—the panic returns.

Writing has been my safe place for so long and where I can lose myself in the most magical way. Anything is possible when writing, and I can let go of my everyday stresses in life. What if I finally share it with someone and lose that? I shudder even thinking about that chance.

Though, it's time to put my fictional worries behind me and focus on the real world. It's Monday and time to get back to editing, the job that I really do enjoy and also pays my bills.

As I walk into work, I wave at Shannon when I pass her desk and she's glowering at her desk while on the phone. I'll have to catch up with her later and see if something happened or if that was just an off moment.

When I get to my office and load my email, I see the most recent one is from Colin. He wants to have a meeting in fifteen minutes.

Shit, I'm supposed to call Gina for a follow up about her edits. I move the mouse to click reply to Colin's message and let him know I'll be late, but then I see something further down from Gina titled "Sick".

Piper,

I know we're supposed to chat today, but I feel like death and you'd probably catch whatever crap this is even through the phone. Seriously, these germs are potent unlike anything I've ever seen.

Reschedule for next week?

Thanks,

G

Well, I guess that solves my problems. Though, I was excited to talk with her. I still think about her story and I'm hoping she's already working on the next book, because I need it almost as badly as I need to have Colin again.

My brows raise at my own thought. Huh. I didn't expect that, but then again, he's charming and handsome and ridiculously sweet. Why wouldn't I want him?

Maybe because he's my boss, I counter inside my mind, then smack my forehead. I am not going to argue with myself right now. That's insane. Right?

With a heavy sigh, I scan through the rest of my email, make my to-do list for the day, then double-check my calendar for the remainder of the week. My biggest thing will be starting the next book from an author I haven't worked with before, but I did enjoy the first read through, so I have high hopes.

Shannon drudges past my office door without looking in. I call her name and she pauses but still isn't smiling.

Quickly, I grab paper and a pen for the meeting, then rush to catch up with her. When I'm at her side, I ask, "Are you okay?"

She holds her stomach and groans. "I think I ate something bad yesterday. Woke up nauseous."

I cringe and take a step back. "Why didn't you stay home?"

"No fever or other symptoms. Pretty sure it was the chicken Matt's mom cooked. I really should stop eating her food. She means well, but man, the kitchen is not the place for her." Shannon's eyes pinch closed, and she sways. "I'll meet you in there."

I watch helplessly as she races back toward the bathroom before I continue on. Poor girl. Maybe I can pop over to the store and get her some crackers or something when the meeting is done.

As my feet carry me closer to the conference room, a tightness forms in my shoulders. Seeing Colin for the first time since we had sex feels awkward. I should have let him stop by yesterday to make today easier, but I hadn't been thinking about today when I'd said I was busy.

Sigh. That's what I get for trying to avoid feelings.

Colin is talking to Brian when I walk in. They're laughing and chatting about some sports game I'm not familiar with, so I take my seat furthest from Colin and get comfortable. Several more minutes tick by while a few others join us, and I listen in on their conversations. I feel a bit like an outsider, since most of them have worked together in other departments for years and Shannon's really the only one who has taken the time to get to know me. Then again, I haven't made an effort with the others.

Even though I've worked for the umbrella company for three years, my company before was completely separate. We only worked on Young Adult books and didn't interact with the other subsidiaries. Now, I wish we had, but I'll find my way here eventually. It's only been a few weeks.

"Is everyone ready to get started?" Colin asks and stands from his spot.

Heads nod throughout the room, and I frown when Shannon still isn't here. "Shannon might be a little longer. She had something to take care of," I say to Colin.

He grins. "Not a problem. I figured at least one person would have issues with a last-minute meeting."

Colin leaves his seat and heads right toward the one next to me at the head of the table. I swallow hard and try not to overreact about his actions. Except, I can't help from wondering why he would do that. Why would he purposely move closer to me? Is he trying to make people think there's something between us?

Then, I see him move his briefcase from the seat. He'd been sitting there before. Holy hell, I'm going to lose my mind keeping our relationship—or whatever this is—a secret.

"So, I know my email was brief, but I met with Steve earlier this morning and we caught up from his business trip out of town. He met with lots of agents and received more queries than the readers can handle right now. There are some that can't wait to be read and responded to, so he's asked me to work with a few of you on getting through the chapters. How is everyone's schedule looking for this week?"

Several frowns appear on faces around the table, but Brian is the first to raise his hand. "I just finished St. Clair's book. I can break for a few days if needed."

I didn't want to be the first to volunteer, but I know I'll have some time this week as well, so I raise my hand next. "I'll help, too."

Shannon walks in with a bright smile on her face and a glimmer in her eyes. The total opposite of how I'd seen her barely five minutes ago.

"What are we volunteering for? Oh, who cares. Count me in," she says chipperly, then squeezes my shoulder as she passes and heads to the empty seat next to Brian.

Interesting.

Colin smiles at all three of us. "Perfect. If you're able to, let's stay after the meeting and get started with a few read-throughs this morning."

Nobody objects, so he continues. "I know we're supposed to have a meeting tomorrow about my observations that have been completed so far, but I figured I'd just fill you all in now while I have you since it won't take long."

Colin opens his briefcase and pulls out a small stack of papers, then starts passing them down. "This is a list of things I noticed that I felt everyone could benefit from and things that more than a few of you were doing that actually costs more of your time. I know I'm not done yet, but the sooner we start to transition, the sooner Steve will be happy with quicker turn-outs on these books."

A few laughs echo around the room. "That man will always want faster returns. He means well, but it's been too many decades since that man has done our job. He forgets what we do," Kasey, the blonde who works on the other side of the office says.

Agreements ring through the room from everyone except me. I haven't seen that side of Steve, so I keep my opinions to myself.

Colin smiles but doesn't outright agree with them. "Review this sheet along with the supporting attachments I'll be sending to your email later this morning. There are trackers and templates that should help all of you. Give them a chance starting today. You won't know how great they can be until you've given them a real try. Though, if there are any tweaks you see that could further add efficiency, don't hesitate to let me know. Any questions?"

Nobody speaks up, but I'm intrigued about the templates and kind of wish I could go back and look at them instead of reading chapters. Oh, well. There will be time later.

Colin dismisses the others and asks Brian and Shannon to move closer to our side of the table. Shannon sits next to me while Brian spreads out next to Colin.

"Alright, so for today, we have six queries that Steve wants back. The rest we'll divide up amongst ourselves and hope that by working on them only a few hours a morning, that we can finish swiftly. They're varying genres, so you might get something you're not used to editing, but try to keep your mind open. If you're unsure about something, let me know and I'll review myself."

Shannon leans forward to grab the packet Colin slides her way. "So, agents were just handing out chapters like candy at the convention he went to?"

Colin shrugs. "I'm not sure where he got all of these, but I do know that a few of the agents they came from, likely the ones we're about to read, represent other authors that could be game-changers for Alliteration. So, we need to be thorough in our reviews. Obviously, we're not going to offer a deal on a book that doesn't deserve one just because we want to get the agent's other clients, but if we can make this a win-win, Steve wants that to happen as soon as possible."

I reach for my papers and frown at my pen. I don't like making edits or notes with ink I can't erase.

"And here are pencils for everyone," Collins says as if he is reading my mind, then puts a handful in between all of us.

As soon as I have one in hand, I immediately dive into the words. The room is quiet while everyone reads, the only noise being the scribble of lead on paper every so often.

That is, until Colin mutters something under his breath, then turns to me. "Can I have your extra rubber?"

I choke on my own spit, and I feel the blood rush straight to my cheeks. "Excuse me?"

Colin's eyes pinch at the sides. "I need a rubber and mine broke."

Between my lack of understanding in what he's trying to say and the sheer embarrassment I suddenly feel from my reaction, I can't form any words in response to his, uh, request.

Finally, he points in front of me. "Your extra pencil, Piper. Can I use the rubber on it?"

Oh, dear lord. The freaking Brit means eraser, and I've just made a fool of myself in front of Brian and Shannon.

"Dude. Rubbers are condoms here. Don't ask women for that. You're lucky she didn't slap you," Brian says with a chuckle.

Oh, thank God. They took my nonsense as being offended.

When I hand Colin the extra pencil I took, he mouths an apology, but I wave him off and gladly go back to my chapter.

Yep. Everything is normal at work now that I've screwed my boss. Totally freaking normal.

Chapter Eighteen

OUT OF EXCUSES

Colin

AFTER THE AWKWARDNESS OF ME ASKING PIPER for an eraser—not a condom—ended, the rest of the time spent reading chapters went better than I expected. From what I had been told, there weren't any group projects before I arrived. That was one of the things I wanted to change.

Yes, the editors needed to work on their own projects, but none of them knew everything. By working together and asking questions like Brian, Shannon, and Piper had been today, they are going to become even better than they are now.

Piper and Shannon just left to get lunch together, a fact that I'm immensely jealous about. As I'm gathering all the papers that were reviewed, Brian stops next to me. "Hey, man. The women can't be the only ones who get to have fun. Want to go grab some food with me?"

I glance at the papers and shake my head. "I need to run these over to Steve, and I don't know how long I'll be."

Brian waves a hand. "No worries. I'll wait."

Well, I can't really say no to that.

"Alright. I'll come to your office when I'm done," I say, then close my briefcase with all the papers I need tucked into a folder.

Brian walks out of the room, and I head in the opposite direction toward Steve's office. It's a corner one with windows on all sides and a view of the city that should be on a postcard especially when the sun is shining like today.

He'd offered me a smaller, similar office across the way, but I'd turn him down, deciding it was better for me to be closer to the other editors.

When I walk in, Steve is sitting behind a mahogany desk, focusing on his computer screen while he types, seemingly unaware of my presence until I clear my throat and knock on the open door.

"Oh, Colin. I'm glad to see you. How are those chapters going?" he asks, pushing glasses I don't often see him wearing higher on his nose.

"Really good actually. Brian, Piper, and Shannon worked with me to get through all of the ones that you said were top priority. There are a few winners in there, but also some that aren't very viable. Notes were left throughout, so you can review them and decide if you want to make any offers," I say while setting my briefcase on his chair and pulling out the folder of already-worked chapters.

Steve holds his hand out and takes the paper from me, grinning so widely that deep wrinkles appear around his face. "Great job. I didn't expect these until the end of the week. Your team must really respect you already to drop what they were doing to do this, and that tells me a lot about how you're doing your job."

I nod stiffly, unsure how to take his praise. "Do you

need anything else? If not, we'll have the rest of these worked through soon."

He flips quickly through a few of them. "I see more notes than I was expecting. Will you be around all day if I have any questions?"

"I was going to go out for lunch, but I can stay just in case." As nice as Brian is, it feels weird getting closer to the other employees when I'm intending to lie to them for as long as I can in order to keep Piper.

He waves a flippant hand in the air. "No, no. You go. I won't be able to get to them for another hour or two anyway."

Well, it looks like I'm out of excuses and off to lunch, then.

———

WITHIN THIRTY MINUTES, I'M SEATED ACROSS from Brian at a sports bar about two blocks from Alliteration. I browse at the menu and decide on pulled pork sliders while Brian orders a bacon burger.

The waiter takes our menus, and I sip my water. The last time I hung out with Brian, we'd both been drinking, so I don't really know what to say. Thankfully, he kicks off the conversation.

"So, how are you feeling about the team so far?" he asks casually.

Okay, maybe not the topic I'm hoping for.

"Everyone I've sat with has been great. I wasn't sure how receptive they'd be to my monitoring them, but overall, I hope the team will all get something from this. If we're all working a similar process and something happens to anyone, it will also make picking up where that person left off easier." My answer is the truth, but the pinched expression on Brian's face says he doesn't understand or possibly believe me.

He takes a long drink from his soda, then asks, "But why change a process that has been working just fine for the ten years I've been here?"

Another question I really don't want to answer, but I do. "Because there can't be growth without change, something that is the only constant in life. Steve shared with me his plans for this part of Alliteration, and I'm just trying to make that happen as smoothly as possible."

Now that gets Brian smiling. "Plans you can share?"

I chuckle and tap my hand on the metal tabletop. "Sure, given you already know that the company wants to continue to grow and increase the market share they hold in publication, they intend to lessen the amount of subsidiaries they own and bring them under the same company. Another big reason why I'm trying to streamline things here is so that when that happens, we have practices in place for the offices that will be going through a full overhaul."

Brian lets out a low whistle but stays quiet as our food arrives.

"Does everything look as ordered?" the server asks, pulling at the collar of his green polo.

"Looks perfect," I answer with a smile.

He quickly heads off to another table, and I return my gaze to Brian. "What do you think about what I shared?"

He picks up his burger with both hands and grins. "I think that I'm one lucky son of a bitch to have not gotten your job."

We both laugh and begin eating in comfortable silence. Maybe this wasn't the worst idea to say yes to lunch.

I finish before Brian and pay the bill for the both of us while he shoves the last two bites into his mouth. When I get my card back, we head out the door and onto the busy sidewalk.

"You know, you're more fun when you're drunk," Brian says with a light tone while we walk.

Feigned hurt crosses my face and I wink. "That was a one-time thing that you can thank Steve for. It was his insistence that got me to that club."

Brian nudges me with his shoulder. "Oh, you know you had fun, so why not do it again?"

"I'm nearing forty. I don't think the club is really my scene anymore," I say with a chuckle.

"But how are you going to meet any ladies when you don't do anything other than work?" He waggles his brows at me before we're forced to separate, thanks to someone on their phone not paying attention to where they're walking.

I clasp his shoulder when we're walking side-by-side again. "I think I can manage on my own. There are parks and coffee shops and plenty of places to meet women. You should remember that for yourself."

He shrugs me off and scoffs. "You just have it easier with that damn accent. That shit is like kryptonite. I wonder if I went to London if my American accent would work the same..."

"Maybe. You're certainly welcome to try," I say with a chuckle while wishing what he'd said about my accent was true. There's one woman who seems to be somewhat immune to it. Though, I respect her desire for taking things slow. Especially when I assume it means she's taking her feelings for me just as seriously as I am for her.

Chapter Nineteen

BIG EGGPLANTS

Piper

WHEN SHANNON ASKED ME TO GO TO LUNCH WITH her, I knew there was no way I could say no with the way she'd walked into that meeting. The need to know what is going on is too strong.

I've asked a dozen times for her to just tell me, but she's refused me every time, saying we had to wait until we were somewhere private.

Now that we're in a booth at the back of a close-by sandwich shop, I plead with her one last time. "Okay, *now* can you tell me what the hell is going on?"

She grins, scans the tables around us, then nods. "I'm pregnant."

My mouth pops open. "How in the world did you figure that out in the short time we were separated?"

I'm pretty sure women—especially first-time moms—don't just *know* when there is a baby growing inside them.

She checks behind us again. "Well, you know how Matt works on the second floor in accounting, right? He'd known how sick I was this morning and told me to stay home. When I told him nothing else was wrong besides having to vomit, he started thinking. After we got to work, the sneaky and very sexy man left and went to the store. He freaking knew before me. Can you believe that?"

No, I actually couldn't. He sounds ridiculously sweet and intuitive and a lot like someone else I've recently met.

"So, he went to the store. Bought crackers and a pregnancy test. Apparently, he told the lady the crackers were either going to help or they weren't." She laughs, and the glow around her has my cheeks aching from smiling so widely. "Anyway, I had texted him on the way to the meeting that if I didn't feel better afterward that I was going home. After leaving you and heading to the bathroom, I found Matt waiting outside the elevator. There he was, holding a paper bag and grinning bigger than the ocean."

My hand covers my chest, and I swoon right alongside her. "That is the sweetest story I think I've ever heard. It could have only been better if you didn't have to find out you were pregnant while at work," I joke.

Her smile fades away. "You can't tell anyone else. I have a strong feeling that things are changing within Alliteration, and if they start canning people, I don't want to be high up on that list."

I lean closer, gripping the menu in front of me with both hands. "What do you mean? They just moved me all the way out here and hired a guy from London to run our department. I thought that meant things were going well."

She shrugs and takes a drink of her water. "It could be a positive change. Either way, I don't want a target on my back until there needs to be one, you know?"

I mean, I didn't know from personal experience, but I can sympathize with where she's coming from. Not all companies enjoyed hiring mothers when they knew their priorities would always be their children and not work.

I don't think Alliteration is like that, but I could be wrong. For Shannon's sake, it's better not to find out the hard way.

We finally order our sandwiches, and while we're waiting, Shannon props her elbows up on the table and rests her chin in her hands. "So, how has LA been treating you so far? I bet our winters are way better than the ones you were used to in North Carolina."

A soft sigh leaves my lips. "I actually love the snow. Though I don't miss it yet, I'm sure by next winter I'll be traveling to go find some. Everything else has been great, though. My condo is perfect for just me. I love that I don't have to commute on any of the highways to get to work and manage to avoid the heavier traffic so many people warned me about."

"You have no idea how lucky you are. I lived in an apartment within walking distance from Alliteration before I met Matt, but it was too small for both of us, so I moved in with him. Biggest mistake ever. I should have just made the man get rid of all his shit. The sometimes-hour-long drive between home and work is asinine." Shannon groans, then takes a drink of her water.

I grimace right alongside her. I couldn't handle that. Maybe I would buy the condo when my rental period came up. Sure, a yard I didn't have to share with someone else would be nice, but dealing with that as opposed to rush hour traffic? Yeah, it didn't sound so bad.

"What about any guys? Have you met anyone worth dating yet? I know Matt has some friends who are single," she says with a spark in her blue eyes.

Outright lying doesn't sit right with me, and I don't

want her trying to set me up with people, so I am as vague as possible. "There's been a few I've seen. One I even went out with, but I'm in no hurry to get into a relationship."

She nods, then backs up as our sandwiches arrive. "You're smart to take things slow. Men can be rather devious around here. Trust your gut if it ever tells you to run for the hills. Don't let million-dollar smiles, dazzling eyes, or big eggplants convince you that your intuition could be wrong."

The young woman who is placing our food on the table snorts, then covers her mouth until her laughter dies down. "Listen to your friend. I've been dating around here for two years. Supposedly there are diamonds in the rough, but I haven't found them yet."

I offer her a sympathetic smile. "Your odds should be going up with every dud, though. So, that's something."

She grins and brushes short ebony strands behind her ear. "That's a good way to see things."

Yeah, maybe. But after hearing what they both said, could I have been so lucky to find a diamond on my first night out in this big city? Seems so unlikely, yet my gut isn't steering me in any other direction.

THE REST OF THE WEEK GOES BY QUICKLY AND before I know it, Friday has arrived. I haven't seen Colin outside of work since the night at his house seven days ago. He hasn't asked to hang out again, and I haven't offered.

The more time that passes, the weirder I feel about things, but Colin continues to act normal with me. Never lingering longer than he should. Never standing closer to me than he does the other employees.

All that makes me happy, but I'm in foreign territory. I have no clue what I'm supposed to do or how to act with him now that we've had sex but can't really date.

Kenzie and Ella have already told me several times to stop overthinking the situation. If he's respecting my space, then that should tell me everything I need to know: he's a keeper.

Except I'm still hung up on what "keeping" him means for my future.

As I sit at my desk, I press my face into my hands and groan. "I just need to go home, open a bottle of wine, and figure the rest out later."

Colin's chuckle echoes into my office. "Well, then. I guess that answers my question."

I peek at him through my fingers, mostly trying to hide my reddening cheeks. "What question is that?"

He steps forward, and I watch how his gray slacks strain against his muscled thighs. His fingertips slide a piece of paper across my desk.

I finally uncover my face and unfold the ripped half-sheet that appears to have come from the notepad I always see him with.

Would you care to join me for game night and drinks? Circle yes or no.

Mother-freaking hell. This man is quickly tearing down the very thick walls I've spent years putting up around me.

Without allowing myself to overthink, I circle yes, then add "my place" to the note before handing it back to him.

He grins widely when he takes the piece of paper and puts it into his front pocket. "I'm leaving for the day. Remember not to work too late and have a good weekend, Piper," he says with a wink before turning to leave my office.

Through my window, I watch him stop by a few other offices before he disappears from sight. I grab my phone and bring up the group chat with Kenzie and Ella.

Me: I'm having game night and drinks at my house with Colin. Do you want to know how he asked me?

Kenzie: Naked and on his knees?

I never thought I'd miss her crassness as much as I do now.

Me: No. With a handwritten note that asked me to circle yes or no.

Ella: That is literally the sweetest thing ever and you're totally getting laid again tonight.

Kenzie: I recommend strip poker to get to that part faster.

Kenzie: Actually, you've now given me an idea. Don't count on me responding for the rest of the night. Bye my favorite bitches. Love you both!

Ella: I sometimes worry Bentley is going to run away from her, but every time I see them together, he's more in love with her than before. Not sure how she does it and probably don't want to know.

Me: No, that information might scar you for life.

Kenzie: Rude. You're just jealous. Now, stop texting and go give both of yourselves a reason not to be.

I actually agree with the crazy woman. Ella must as well, because I don't hear from either of them again as I gather my things to head home.

Once I'm in my car, I realize I volunteered my place, but Colin is the one with a pet and he must have already bought games. It would probably be easier if I went to his house, so I text him as much.

Colin: I can bring the games and drinks to your place and I'll feed Charlie before I go. He'll be fine for the night.

Me: If you're sure it's not too much trouble...

Colin: I'm more than sure.

His reply comes quickly, and I'm near giddy as I start my car, then pull out of the parking garage.

This is going to be a great night. There will be no overthinking. Only laughter, good company, and even better sex.

Chapter Twenty

NEVER HAVE I EVER

Colin

I'VE CHANGED MY TROUSERS TWICE, MY SHIRT four times, and now I'm debating between my Converse or something nicer for shoes.

I shouldn't be so nervous. Nothing has gone wrong this week. Well, except for Piper keeping her distance ever since we slept together. Maybe I shouldn't have let things go so far, but it's too late to dwell on that now.

She at least said yes to the date night. That's what I need to focus on.

Wanting to be more comfortable than fashionable, I put on my black Converse and give Charlie a long scratch on the head. "I'll be back later tonight. Well, maybe. If I'm not, I'll be here first thing in the morning to feed you. If you scratch the sofa again while I'm gone, we're going to have words."

He meows and rubs his nose against my hand. Maybe the cat isn't so terrible all the time.

I leave him on my bed and head toward the garage. The

car is already loaded with games and drinks. I'm probably bringing too many options, but I don't know what Piper likes—at least, not yet—and that will hopefully change after tonight.

The drive to her house is short, and I almost park in her driveway, but instead, I turn around and park on the corner to her street. She doesn't have a two-car garage like I do, and I'm not asking her to move her vehicle out to hide mine.

I gather the games I think will be the biggest hits, like a couple of card games based on Never Have I Ever and Two Truths and a Lie, then the classic Sorry and Monopoly. I figure if she chooses one of the first two, then she's just as intrigued about me as I am her. If she sticks with the latter, then I've still got a lot more work to do in winning her trust.

Once all of the games are stacked under one arm, I grab the bag of drinks and head for Piper's house. It's the second condo in the row of four with vibrant green yards and minimal flowers. The exterior is a sage green. When I get to the white front door, I glance behind me to make sure none of the neighbors are out. There's no telling how many other employees live over here.

"Coming," Piper's faint voice sounds through the door after I knock.

A smirk grows on my face. I hope she will be later.

The deadbolt turns and I straighten my shoulders, eagerly waiting to see Piper's sweet face on the other side.

She opens the door with a huff and gestures for me to step in. "Sorry. I was making brownies."

The chocolatey scent wafts around her, and I take a deep inhale. "Smells delicious."

A flush covers her cheeks. "I also grabbed chips and

salsa, a veggie tray, and put crackers and cheese on a platter. I was nervous and needed to keep busy."

Her honesty takes me by surprise and has my chest tightening. I reach over and set the items I've brought in down on the long entry table behind her.

When I step back to Piper, I pull her into my arms and squeeze. "Would it make you feel better to know that I changed clothes more than a few times?"

She nods against my shoulder. "It does, actually." Then, she releases me. "Since you weren't here long the first time, let me give you a tour. A real one. Not like the one you gave me. Not that there was anything wrong with yours. I mean... I'm going to shut up now."

I chuckle as she tries to hide her rosy cheeks from me, then reach to intertwine her fingers with mine. "It's okay, Piper. There are no expectations tonight."

Okay, maybe I'm lying a little. There are definite hopes for how this evening ends, but there's no pressure she needs to worry about. I hope she knows that.

She finally smiles up at me and squeezes our combined hands. "Thank you."

We continue down the small hallway, and it opens up into a cozy living room with cream-colored walls and bright paintings hung up. Brown couches take up a lot of the floor space, then there's a big screen on the wall above a propane fireplace.

Up ahead is the kitchen and a small yet tall pub table that has four chairs but is probably better suited for three.

"Snacks on the counter for whenever you're hungry," she says, then laughs. "This seems self-explanatory, but here's the kitchen and we just passed the family room."

I grin. "Very lovely. You've already made this home in just a few weeks."

She shrugs, then pulls me along. We go back past the living room and through a shorter hallway. She points at the first door. "Bathroom there and a storage closet after that. Please don't get them confused."

A chuckle builds in my chest. "Has that happened in the short time you've lived here?"

She shakes her head and frowns. "No, but my friends will be here in two weeks, and I'm worried it might then, so I decided to make it a habit to remind people when I give the tours."

"How many tours have you given?" I raise a brow and hope none recently.

Her grip tightens on my hand that she's still holding. "Just Shannon and you."

Well, that makes me feel better. Though, I wish I had been the first.

We continue to a set of stairs at the end of the hallway. They lead to a small landing with three more doors. She points to each one, beginning with the first on our right. "That's my office-slash-guest room, then the bathroom that also has a door to lead into my room, which is on the left."

Her office door is cracked open, and I nod toward it. "Do I get to see where you work when you're not at Alliteration?"

She hesitates, then says, "Sure. It's nothing special, given the lack of room I have here."

I follow her into the space, and the first thing I notice is the bunk beds. "Interesting choice."

"You'll understand more when you meet Kenzie and Ella," she says, then her face blanches. "I mean, this is if you still want to while they're here."

I jerk her toward me, placing our still combined hands

against my chest. "I would love to meet the women you talk so much about."

She smiles, and I can't wait any longer. I lean forward, pressing my mouth to hers. Her tongue barely peeks out and I don't miss the opportunity to part her lips with mine.

As much as I want to continue, with as distant as Piper has been all week, I force myself back, then glance at her desk. There are two monitors on a wooden surface that take up half of the surface, and I notice her laptop is missing from the docking station. In the middle is a keyboard that's covered by printed chapter pages.

"I thought you stopped printing for edits," I tease and reach for the sheets.

She smacks my hand away. "Those are, um, old. Come on. I need to cut the brownies before they, uh, get cold."

Interesting. I thought it was better to cut them when they were cooler, but then again, I'm not a baker and don't question her. Piper releases my hand and gives me a nudge back out the door and closes it behind her while I go down the stairs first.

I make my way to the kitchen and lean against the counter before grabbing one of the crackers and a slice of cheese. "Thanks for thinking of food."

She nibbles at her lower lip and nods while pulling a knife from one of the drawers next to the oven.

Instead of letting the awkwardness from her office linger, I decide we need a distraction. "I'm going to go grab the games and get one set up. I have two card games: Never Have I Ever and Two Truths and a Lie. I also brought Monopoly and Sorry if you like longer games. Which one?"

Piper's eyes don't leave the brownies until she finally answers me. "Never Have I Ever."

It isn't until I've moved out of eyesight from her that I

let the grin grow across my face. Tonight is going to be even better than I expected.

By the time I have the box opened and cards organized, Piper enters the living room with a plate between her hands that's filled with a little of everything that she has out on the counter. "Do any of the drinks you brought need to go in the fridge?"

"Only the wine. I brought a red and white since I wasn't sure what you preferred," I answer, then add, "Or, you're welcome to the whiskey I also brought."

She reaches for the bag sitting next to me on the couch and takes it with her back to the kitchen. I expect her to return with a wine glass and whatever she has for my whiskey, but instead, she has two glass tumblers and the now-open bottle in hand.

I don't comment on her drink choice. Instead, I begin to explain the rules of the game, adding a few of my own and tossing out the rule cards when they seem to complicate things more than I think tonight needs.

"So, we'll take turns drawing cards from this stack. If you've done what's on your card, then you lay it down in front of you and take a drink. Once you have ten guilty cards, then you win. No skips or pleading the fifth as you Americans like to say. If you really don't want to answer, you drink anyway and I get to assume the answer. We'll take turns drawing cards from the pile. And just to keep things interesting, if we're both guilty, we both drink."

While biting at the inside of her cheek, she glances at the whiskey, then at the stacks of cards.

"You can change to the wine if you'd rather," I offer with a smile.

Her head shakes stiffly. "Honestly, I'm wishing I'd chosen Sorry, but no, this is good."

"Are you sure? I can get the board game out." I'm not about to push this divine woman away over a stupid card game.

She nods and meets my gaze. "Absolutely. I'll go first." She picks up a card, then snorts. There's a spark in her eyes and a smile lifting on her lips. "Never have I ever bought tampons."

A pout immediately lands on my face. "That is a horrible card."

She takes the bottle and pours both of us a drink before lifting her glass toward those perfect lips of hers. "You bought the game. I just agreed to play." Then, she takes a longer pull than I expect and doesn't even cough when she sets the glass back down.

To say I'm shocked and even more intrigued is an understatement.

I grab the next card and laugh. "Never have I ever been skinny dipping." My eyes watch her hand, and when she reaches for her glass, I tilt my head in interest while taking my own drink.

"Seriously. You'll understand more in a couple weeks. Kenzie is a special breed," Piper answers my unasked question. I merely nod while she goes again.

Her face goes pale, and I'm sure she's about to bow out, but a few seconds later, she finally reads the card. "Never ever have I had sex with someone whose name I didn't know."

Piper's green eyes watch my hand, but I don't lift my glass. That's something I've never done and don't intend to do in the future either.

Then, I see her drink lift, and my mouth pops open. "Oh, do tell, and you can't blame this one on your friend, either."

She finishes the sip and shakes her head. "Nope. That's not part of the game. I can admit to anything, but you don't get the details."

"Damn, I should have amended more of the rules," I say with feigned hurt.

Piper's smile lights up the room as I pull the next card. This is exactly what we needed, and I'm going to make sure we get through this whole deck before the night is over or the whiskey is gone.

Chapter Twenty-One

A LITTLE CROOKED

Piper

THE WHISKEY BOTTLE IS NEARLY GONE. MY EYES can see that, but my brain doesn't quite compute what that means. At least, not yet.

I'm having too much fun with Colin to care if I'm more than a little drunk. The only things that matter are that the room isn't spinning and I don't have the sudden need to run for the toilet.

The seemingly never-ending deck of Never Have I Ever cards is finally dwindling, but we seem to have stopped picking them up and have begun making up our questions.

"Never have I ever wore men's underwear," I say with a giggle, then hiccup as my laughter grows.

Colin glares at me. "You're trying to purposefully get me sloshed, aren't you?"

Using my pointer finger, I draw an imaginary halo around my head. "I'd never."

His English accent is really coming out now, and it's

making him even hotter, but at this point, the sex is probably going to be drunk and sloppy and... Okay, maybe that's not so bad.

"My turn," he demands. "Never have I ever...um, shit, we've been playing this for too long to remember what's already been done. Uh, never have I ever wanted to be anything other than an editor."

His hand smacks his forehead, and he takes a small sip from the tumbler. "I clearly didn't think that one through."

I'm mid-sip and some of the whiskey dribbles down my chin. "No, you should have said never have I ever had a vagina."

His face blanches, then he laughs so hard I'm not even sure he can breathe properly. "You said vagina."

Now, it's my turn to smack my forehead. "Yes, you know that part of me that your dick loves so much. I wouldn't laugh too hard at that."

He sobers quickly and winks at me. "Yes, ma'am. Let's go back to my question. What did you want to be if not an editor? Let me guess. A princess."

My head shakes, and then I groan from the action, pushing my glass further. I know when enough is enough. "Nope, not that. A writer—I mean. No, that's not right. Um, a...I don't know."

Oh, God. I just told this man my darkest secret. The one not a single soul on this earth knows. Yeah, I'm definitely done drinking now.

Colin's head cocks to the side, and his eyes squint at me. "A writer? You know when I first sat with you, I thought you had the passion for writing. Glad to see I was accurate in my observation. Have you written anything?"

I shake my finger at him since that's safer than my head.

"No, I didn't say *writer*. I said raider like *Tomb Raider*. Totally wanted to be her when I grew up."

Intoxicated brain for the win. I have no clue how I just pulled that one out of my ass.

"I don't believe you, and I think it's great you want to write." He pauses, and it's almost as if his light-gray eyes pierce my soul for the briefest second. "You shouldn't be ashamed of your dreams. You should embrace them."

Damn it. Why did he have to say that? Why does he have to make me feel so much with just his words and the way he looks at me? I can't tell if it's my inebriated state or how much I'm beginning to care about this man, but I suddenly have word vomit unlike ever before.

"I have embraced them. A lot, actually. Though, only privately, and I've never finished a full book. Only short fanfics or partial plots that I was too afraid to complete for fear that I might actually want to share them with anyone who could ruin the escape that my writing is for me. It's a stress relief unlike anything I've ever done. A way to channel emotions that might not be acceptable to express otherwise."

Colin reaches for me, giving my thigh a soft squeeze, and my already-racing heart feels like it's about to rip from my chest. "Thank you for sharing that with me. With as badly as you're shaking right now, I don't imagine that was easy."

I snort-laugh. "Being intoxicated helps, but I'll probably regret this in the morning. No offense to you, it's just I haven't even told my best friends and now they'll probably kill me for telling you first."

He winks at me. "I'll be sure to save you from any murderous attempts they plan to make on your life."

I giggle and swoon dramatically, batting my lashes up at him and holding a hand to my chest. "I don't know what I'd do without you."

Colin holds tighter to my leg, then grabs my waist with his other hand. I suddenly find myself moving over the cards. Before I can even get a squeal out, I'm sitting in his lap.

"Is that sarcasm I sense, Ms. Fitz?" he murmurs against my ear.

I smirk. "Maybe."

"Maybe I need to show you my hidden talents, so you believe I'm capable of keeping you safe," he says with a low growl in his voice.

Heat unfurls deep within me and spreads throughout my body as I shamelessly wiggle over his lap. "Or, you could just have your way with me, and we could pretend this conversation never happened."

His responding grin makes my skin tingle, and I reach for his outstretched hand. When his fingers grip my wrist to help me up, he whispers, "No amount of whiskey could make me forget this night, Piper, but I will gladly have my way with you."

Oh, God. What have I done? I don't know and I don't even think it's a bad thing, but am I ready for this? Am I ready for the big feelings Colin evokes from me? I'm not sure, but I don't want to stop our night.

I need him too much right now.

"Then, let's go upstairs," I say when I'm finally on two feet and leaning against his chest.

Now that we're both standing, the alcohol seems to be hitting me harder. I sway more than I expect, but Colin uses the couch to help keep us upright and we carefully make our way to the stairs.

Between the two of us, we manage to turn off all the lights as we go, double-check the door is locked, and get upstairs with only one near-death episode while traversing the suddenly precarious steps.

By the time we get to my bedroom, all the previous seriousness is gone and we're laughing our asses off when I ask how my shirt is somehow half off and why Colin's pants are unbuttoned, barely staying up.

"What can I say? I'm desperate for naked time, love. I need to see your tits more than I need...water," Colin says. I try not to allow my chest to tighten once again at his casual use of the pet name "love."

Though, his mention of water does remind me that we both need to take something for our heads or we will be hating life when the sun rises.

"Hold those 'tit' thoughts." Before he can stop me, I head into my bathroom and open the drawer, knowing I have pain medicine here for when my cramps aren't playing nice.

I grab two pills for each of us and fill up the plastic cup I keep on my sink with tap water. Not the best, but it's better than risking the stairs again.

I drink the whole cup while downing the pills then quickly refill when I can hear Colin grunting in the other room. Though, my rush is more out of curiosity than concern.

My brain can't compute what my eyes are seeing when I get back into the bedroom. Colin's arms are trapped in his shirt. His shoes are still on and stuck inside his jeans, and he's bent over my mattress with his boxer-brief-covered ass in the air.

I have to cover my mouth to stifle the laughter bubbling

inside me that only gets louder when he mutters, "Help a bloke out."

"I'm not even sure where to start," I choke out, my shoulders still shaking from the giggles.

His head turns sideways. "Are you laughing at me? I'm going to smack that sweet arse of yours when I get out of this mess."

His voice is deep and hot, and the thinly veiled threat sobers me slightly.

My feet move of their own accord. After setting the glass and pills down, I work on his shirt first so that he can have his arms back. I'm not even sure where the holes are at this point, but I begin tugging with an enthusiasm I didn't have moments ago.

"Someone's a little eager to get spanked, aren't they?" Colin takes a deep inhale. "I can smell you already."

Oh, hell. Why does that turn me on even more?

"I thought I was going to have to ease you into some things, but maybe I was wrong to assume..." Colin adds, further making my task at hand much harder than it should be.

"Please, stop talking until we're both naked," I beg, my voice raspy and breathy.

The smirk on his face nearly makes me regret my words, but not quite. I finally get his arms free, and the shirt gets flung across the room. When my fingers attempt to yank on his jeans, my arms are pulled back up. Before I know what's happening, Colin has me pinned against the bed.

The grin he's giving me makes my pussy clench with anticipation unlike anything ever has. "How's this for having my way with you? I'm going to tie your hands to that headboard while making you scream loud enough to make your neighbors jealous."

His words cause a heavy wave of pleasure to douse me, and I swallow thickly. "Yes, please."

Colin grabs my chin and kisses me hard before backing up and getting his pants off all on his own.

While he's busy with that, I get naked quicker than ever, uncaring that my clothes are being tossed all over the room. I can clean tomorrow. Tonight is about getting fucked. Literally.

Once all of our clothes have been disbanded, Colin heads for my dresser. "Where are your scarfs, assuming you don't have any silk ties lying around?"

I point to the third drawer. "There."

He opens it and pulls out two of them. One bright red one and one black one. "These will work good enough for tonight."

Who is this man, and where is the light-hearted and patient man I've been getting to know? Just kidding. I don't really care. I'm too damned curious about the sexy beast stalking toward me with an intent in his eyes that I'm not sure how to read but sure the hell thrilled to see.

The rise and fall of my chest quickens, and my knees tremble next to each other.

"Get on the bed, Piper. Move close to the headboard and spread your arms out." His demand is fuel to an already raging inferno inside of my body.

Nobody has ever talked to me like this in bed. Nobody has ever tied my hands. Nobody has nearly made me come just from words.

Nobody until Colin.

Holy hell. I am so screwed.

Without hesitation, I do as he says and wrap my fingers around the wooden slats behind me. Colin walks to the left side of the bed, using the red scarf first. I watch his every move as he reaches down to my shoulder, leaves a burning trail of ecstasy along my arm with his fingers, then wraps the soft material around my wrist before securing it to the headboard.

"Is that okay?" he asks.

The question surprises me considering his demeanor just a moment ago, but I still nod in reply.

He leans over the bed and captures my lips. "I need words, Piper."

"Yes, it's okay," I whisper with his face still close to mine.

He kisses me once more, and I reach over with my right hand to hold him to me, but he's gone before I can grab on to him.

There's a wicked smile on his face as he walks to the other side of the bed. I cross my ankles, pressing my legs tighter together, trying to ease the buildup growing inside me.

I don't see him move closer, but suddenly, he's whispering in my ear, "Be grateful you don't have a footboard that I can tie your ankles to as well."

Shit, he needs to stop speaking and start acting right the fuck now.

Between the alcohol, his voice, my neediness, and everything he's already doing, I'm so close to slipping over the edge. The need to do so is nearing painful.

Then, I ask a question that I only have the courage to ask because of the whiskey still racing through me. "Are you a Dom? Do I have to call you Sir?"

His chuckle runs through me as if the sound physically touches my skin and sets me on fire. "No to both questions, but I do like to think outside the proverbial box. Often."

The slight wave of disappointment that hits me shocks

the hell out of my mind. I'm not this woman. I'm not adventurous, or a sex fiend, or...a submissive. Why would his answer make me frown?

Maybe I don't really know myself and Colin is about to show me what I've been missing out on all these years of being reserved.

After securing my other wrist, he walks to the front of the bed and disappears from sight when he bends down. I watch until he stands again, rolling a condom onto his hard, much-too-big cock.

Air presses down on me and the need to bring my arms down hits me hard, except I can't and I'm not sure yet how that makes me feel.

Colin spreads my legs, then grabs each ankle, gently pulling me forward until my body is taut. My skin feels like it's near melting temperature, and he's barely even touched me.

"See why I like to do things differently, my little bird? Nothing crazy or rough or torturous, but adventurous if you're willing," Colin says as he moves onto the bed.

"Yep. Willing participant right here," I pant. I just need him to freaking touch me so I can ignite properly.

He bends down, and I lose sight of his head from my position, but the feel of his tongue dragging up my pussy is not something I could miss.

My hips lift on their own, forcing his tongue closer to where I need it, and I cry out from the not-quite relief.

Just when I think he's going to pull back to draw things out, Colin's mouth covers my clit and sucks hard.

The one action has me falling hard and screaming. My thighs tighten around his head, and I hear the creak of wood behind me when my arms attempt to flail.

The bite of pain at my wrist only adds to the ecstasy

racing through my body as Colin continues to ravage my pussy.

Once the wave of the orgasm dies down, he lifts his head, but before he can say anything, I mutter a "thank you" without any shame.

He chuckles, grabbing both of my hips with his hands. "We're just getting started, love."

Before I can ask what's next, he answers the unspoken question by lifting my legs and rubbing his cock against my clit. "Don't forget to relax or I won't be able to get in that tight cunt of yours."

I glare at him. "How am I supposed to relax when you're doing *that*?"

Colin crawls over me, and I keep my legs wrapped around his waist. His lips press against mine, and he gently strokes the skin around my neck and collarbone with the tips of his fingers until I feel like I'm melting into the bed.

His tongue demands entrance into my mouth, and I'm shocked when I'm not repulsed by my own taste. As Colin continues to kiss me deeply and drag his fingers over my over-sensitized skin, I finally feel his dick sliding into me.

That sneaky Brit. Though, I really have no reason to complain. I'm getting what I so desperately needed.

Thankfully, it doesn't take nearly as long this time as the first. Within a minute, Colin is fully seated inside me, moving more fluidly and already beginning to work me up again.

He rises up, using his arms for support while his hips do all the work down lower. His gaze traps mine, and I can't look away from him while he pounds into me, soft yet firm and full of powerful emotions.

His eyes are like a window into his soul, and he's not

even trying to hide the feelings he's showing me through his acts of tenderness and patience.

As my thoughts begin to spiral, so do my own emotions, and the walls of my pussy are starting to clamp down around him.

"Not yet, little bird. I'm not done showing you how good this can be." He moves me higher up onto the bed until my head is nearly touching the headboard.

My arms are thankful for the relief of pressure I hadn't even been noticing, but before I can enjoy the relief for too long, Colin pulls out of me, then quickly flips me over until I'm resting on my knees and gripping the wooden slats with my now-crossed arms.

"Are you okay like that?" he asks, voice thick and grumbly.

I nod my head, then add a "yes" when I remember he likes words, not gestures.

His palm smacks my ass. "Good."

Colin runs a finger between my cheeks, then parts my folds before entering me again.

My head drops down, and I hold on for dear life as he pounds into me like a king owning his queen. One of his hands grips my hair, and I'm forced to look up, causing my back to arch more.

"Feels so fucking good being inside you," he mutters, and I badly wish I could see his face.

This position has him driving deeper inside me. I didn't think that was even possible after the first time we had sex.

I'm dripping for him and can feel the wetness trailing down my thighs as my next orgasm builds bigger and faster than the one prior.

"Oh, hell," I grunt, resting my head against the headboard. "Nearly there."

"I'm well aware, love." I can hear the confident grin in his voice as his speed increases. I'm helpless to do anything other than hold on for dear life and hope I don't die from the fierce energy ripping through my body right now.

Colin's hold on my hair and hip gets tighter, and little grunts sound from the back of his throat, telling me my orgasm will likely push him over the edge.

I push back against him, sending his cock further inside me, then cry out, as my body succumbs to the shudders taking over. Unable to hold on to the headboard, my face falls into the pillow below and captures my screams of ecstasy.

All sense of awareness for my surroundings is gone for at least a minute until I feel a tug at my awkwardly twisted wrists.

When I manage to turn my head, Colin is getting the first scarf off, and I can see his condom-covered dick resting against the comforter. The protection might be filled with cum, but that man is still more than half hard. Yet, there's no way I can do *all* that again.

He moves to the other side and undoes the final restraint, but I don't move. I just let my arms sink into the bed and groan. "I'm never going to be able to walk again."

His soft chuckle carries through the room. "Yes, you are. Maybe just a little crooked for a day or two, though."

He's still laughing as he heads toward the bathroom. Then, I manage to roll over and say, "This better not happen every time or we're only having sex on Fridays."

Colin stops in the doorway and winks. "You better have a proper conversation with your vagina and tell her to get used to the attention, because once a week might not be enough—" he glances down, "—for him."

I throw an arm over my face and groan. Mostly because he's right. Once a week isn't enough for either of us. I can't deny this man, even if I should.

Work be damned, I feel too good to walk away from him now.

Chapter Twenty-Two

LITTLE BIRD

Colin

THE NEXT MORNING, THE SUN IS UP, AND I SWEAR I hear the birds singing. Even if the sound is in my head, I couldn't care less. When I look over and see Piper's angelic face on the pillow next to me, my chest expands, and a grin grows on my face.

My arm is draped over her as she sleeps on her back. I gently lift up and roll to the edge of the bed. Once I'm on my feet, I glance back and see she's still sound asleep, which is unsurprising, given how much we drank last night. Damn, it was worth every drop of burning whiskey down my throat.

She had been so open and carefree while we played the ridiculous yet eye-opening card game. Then, in bed? Bloody hell, I've never had better sex.

I grab my boxer briefs from the floor, and when I'm nearly done putting them on, my ankle rolls and I crash into the dresser. My hands catch me, but slam into an open laptop. A quick look back finds Piper still sleeping soundly. Though, I'm not sure how.

I give the dresser a once-over to make sure I didn't ruin any of the items she has on there, like a few pictures of her and her friends and the candles placed between them. I slide a few things back into place, then notice her laptop screen is now on, open to the beginning of a chapter.

My eyes cast over the words, and before I know it, I'm reaching to scroll down on the screen to find out what happens next. Except, I stop myself when I remember what Piper told me last night.

She likes to write. This could be her own words and not something from work. Continuing feels like an invasion of privacy, a line I shouldn't cross. Though, I can't deny I really want to know what happens next.

Her work, if my assumption is right, is damn good. She should be proud of what she has here. I don't know if she would be okay with me saying so, though. Hell, I don't even know if she'll remember telling me her secret last night.

If she does, maybe I'll ask about the woman in the woods being hunted by a wolf. Her fear felt so tangible on the pages that even my own spiked.

I double-check everything is back where it was on the dresser, then head downstairs to cook breakfast. That is, if I can find everything that I need to make some omelets or maybe even French toast.

When I enter the kitchen, I quietly open as many cabinets as it takes to find what I need. Bread, cinnamon, syrup, pans, milk, and eggs are all sitting on the counter next to the stove as I get the burner turned on.

I make four slices of French toast first, followed by some

scrambled eggs, a last-minute addition in case she hates French toast for some reason.

Once I have both plates served, I snag the syrup and remember we'll need something to drink. I put everything down and check the fridge again. She has a few bottles of water on the bottom shelf, so I grab two, shoving them under my arms then grabbing the other items again.

Carefully, I make my way back up the stairs and find Piper sitting up in bed. "I was one second from coming down there until I heard you coming up the stairs," she says with a groan and a rub of her stomach.

Before I hand her plate over, I lean forward and capture her lips. "Good morning, little bird."

Her brows furrow, and she steals the food from my hand. "Good morning and thank you, but also why do you call me that now?"

I grin and get settled on the bed with her before answering. "The way you keep yourself guarded reminds me of how a bird keeps its wings close, but when they're ready to soar, those feathers unfurl into something so beautiful. Just how I see you, especially after getting to know you better last night."

She blushes and stares hard at her food. "Okay. I wasn't expecting that."

I chuckle. "A little too much this early in the day?"

Piper finally looks up, and there's a small smile on her face. "Maybe." She takes her first bite of French toast and moans. "Holy hell, this is delicious. Why is it so good?"

"I could lie and say because I'm an amazing cook, but I don't want future expectations to be too high. It's more likely because you're hungover from the whiskey." I can still smell the alcohol on me, and as much as I don't want to leave Piper, I'm ready to shower and change.

She sighs and takes another bite, then says, "There was a lot of drinking last night."

"Do you have any regrets?" I ask with a raised brow. My stomach churns waiting for her answer.

"Not a one." She grins. "Do you?"

I let out a relieved sigh. "Nope."

We eat in comfortable silence until she drops her fork, and it clatters onto the glass plate. "Uh, I might have one regret."

Hesitantly, I ask, "What would that be?"

"I told you something I've never told anyone else before," she says quietly and without looking at me.

"About your writing? You have nothing to be embarrassed about there. The joy on your face as you talked about it is something everyone should experience in their lifetime," I say sincerely. "Don't ever feel like you have to hide who you are around me or anyone else."

With her sudden uncertainty, I'm tempted not to tell her what I saw on her laptop, but I don't want there to be any lies between us. Not when we already have so many other obstacles to overcome if things for us are going to work.

As she moves the eggs around on her plate, I finally add, "I have something I should tell you."

Her eyes snap up to meet mine, a bit of hope inside them. "A dark secret to share?"

My head shakes and I keep my smile small. "Not exactly. When I was getting dressed this morning, I bumped into your dresser and knocked some things around. Your laptop might have turned on and I might have read some of the words there."

She flicks her gaze to the screen, then back to me. "No."

Then, her shoulders go rigid and the color drains from her cheeks.

I reach a hand to her and offer a small squeeze. "I stopped when I realized it might not be something from work. I didn't mean to invade your privacy, but I was sucked in and still wish I could read more. I haven't lied to you, and I don't intend to start now, so when I say this, I want you to know I'm telling the truth."

I pause, waiting for her to give any inclination that she'd rather I just shut the hell up, but when her eyes peek up at me, waiting and full of trepidation, I continue, "Those words are bloody brilliant, little bird. In just a few paragraphs, you made me feel every emotion that Ember was as she ran through that forest and the need to know what happens to her next is ridiculously strong. Even now."

Her eyes widen, and she shakes her head while her hands grip her knees through the comforter over her legs. "I've literally never told anyone in the entire world that I like to write before last night. Well, not unless you count the squirrel that used to frequent my backyard. I just do it for fun and as a stress reliever."

I lean forward and cup her cheek. "Thank you for allowing me to be the first human to know. That means a lot to me. And I'm sorry if my reading those words upset you, but now that I know...I'd really like to read more. Whenever you're ready."

Piper's cheeks blush and she tries to turn away, but I force her to look back at me.

"Seriously. You're very talented. If you haven't already, I hope you finish that book. Ember deserves to have her story told."

"You really think so?" she asks, eyes wide and bright.

I press my lips to hers for a brief second. "I know so." I

grab her plate and pile it on top of mine. "I'll let you get up while I take these downstairs to clean up the mess, then I'll head home."

Piper glances at the clock and lightly covers her mouth with her hand. "Charlie! He's been alone all night."

"And he's perfectly fine. He has a litter box and a mound of food he probably hardly touched. I promise," I say solemnly.

"Next time, maybe you can bring him here," she replies, and my heart soars.

I didn't cross a line big enough to push her away. She said "next time," and I'm going to hold on to that promise until it comes to fruition, which I bloody hope is before next Friday.

———

AFTER I DO THE DISHES AND CLEAN UP MY MESS from breakfast—much to Piper's dismay—I leave her with a branding kiss while keeping her pinned against the wall by the front door.

Our tongues are even more acquainted, and her chest is heaving by the time I say my goodbyes. With a bright smile on my face, I walk down the block to my car and hop in. Within a couple minutes, I'm home and Sir Charles is screaming at me from the kitchen.

When I walk inside from the garage, he's on the counter and pawing at his wet food bowl that's nearly to the edge of the counter.

"You do realize that you're not actually royalty, right? There is still more than half of your food left in the bowl down there. I don't even want to hear your complaints," I say while reaching into the cabinet to get the spoiled furball exactly what he wants.

Okay, maybe Piper isn't the only one with a soft spot for the feline.

After appeasing Charlie, I go straight to the shower, but before I get in, I grab my phone and text Piper.

Me: Thank you for letting me stay the night and for sharing a part of yourself with me. I don't take that lightly.

After I hit send, I realize that could be taken the wrong way and I hope she knows I'm talking about the book and not the sex. Though, that was just as fantastic, but in a different way. Much different.

Piper: Thanks for not making me feel like a fool for hiding that part of me. It's been a long time since I've felt this way. I don't take that lightly, either.

There is so much I could say to that, but I don't want to push her with a heavy text conversation, so I keep things light.

Me: Good. We're going to find a way to make this work. For now, we trade weekends at our places?

*Piper: I look forward to our next sleepover *heart eye emoji**

Fuck. So do I.

I put my phone down and step into the shower. As soon as the steaming water hits my skin, my brain begins to process everything that's happened in the last month since meeting Piper.

Things might not be so easy for us, thanks to work, but maybe it doesn't have to be that complicated.

Maybe we already have the answer we need, and we didn't even realize it.

Chapter Twenty-Three

KINKY SHIT

Piper

HOLY HELL. I DON'T KNOW HOW TO PROCESS what has happened over the last twelve hours, but nothing is what I expected. Well, except for the sex. I knew that would be amazing, just like the first time. But everything else? All I can think is, *What did I do?*

Not in a bad way. I'm doing what I set out to do when I moved out here. I wanted to be a new me who didn't hold back in life. Opening up to Colin, telling him my deepest secret—which shouldn't even be a secret—is good.

Yet, I also feel terrible that Ella and Kenzie weren't the first people to know about my writing. Now I need them to know right away. Otherwise, the guilt will eat away at my soul until they do.

Me: SOS. Video chat?

Ella: Two minutes.

Kenzie: Oh, you know Owen only needs one.

I snort at Kenzie's text, then head to the bathroom and

make sure I don't look recently ravaged. That woman doesn't need any more ammunition to be inappropriate.

After running a brush through my hair, I head downstairs, and my phone starts ringing just as I enter the kitchen.

The video loads, and Kenzie joins in at the same time as me but doesn't get a chance to speak before Ella glares at the screen. "Owen says you owe us another apology gift for that comment."

Kenzie throws her head back as she laughs, her auburn hair cascading behind her. "Ha. Not going to happen. He never even thanked me for the first one, which I *know* he enjoyed."

"Ella," I hear Owen's growling tone in the background.

She looks away from the screen. "Oh, come on. You can't tell me all of your conversations with Bentley are innocent. You know there are no secrets between the three of us."

I internally cringe at Ella's words. Well, there won't be any others as soon as we get to have this conversation.

Owen's laugh sounds sinister. "So, they know about last week when we—"

Ella's eyes widen, and she throws a pillow from their bed. "Get out. Now."

His chuckle follows him out of the room, and Kenzie is staring at Ella with all the interest in the world showing through her eyes. "So, what have you whores been up to? Between the SOS and Owen's comment, I feel like this is going to be the best conversation ever."

I mean, she's probably not wrong, but I don't tell her that.

Ella's cheeks are flushed, and she forces a grin to her

face. "Owen was just trying to start some shit. Nothing happened last week."

Kenzie's hand slams down on something hard, possibly her nightstand. "Bullshit. We know you better than that. Just like I know Piper has something juicy to say. Since hers will probably take longer, you better spill the tea and tell us what kinky shit you did with your husband. No judgement. Only curiosity over here."

I shrug at Ella's panicked look. "I have to side with Kenzie here. Your reaction is only making it so that we *have* to know. I mean, it's not like you had a threesome or something. It can't be that crazy."

Ella gulps, and my eyes bulge, but it's Kenzie who responds first. "If you fucked another woman and it wasn't me, I think my feelings are actually going to be hurt."

I can't stop the laughter that rips through me. My entire body shakes, and I nearly drop the phone onto the tile floor in the kitchen.

When I gain control of myself, Ella is covering her face and shaking her head. "I didn't have sex with another woman. We didn't invite another partner into our bed, but Owen might have, um, well, fuck. Wedidanal."

Her words are spoken so quickly that they sound like only one was said, but all we needed to hear to understand was that last bit: anal.

Kenzie frowns and then lets out a huff. "Seriously? How is it that you've done that before me? Damn it. Now I need to get fucked in the ass so we can chat about this properly. I mean, don't get me wrong, there's been some serious finger play, but actual dick penetration? Not so much. Now, though? I'll bring the idea up. How was it? Did it hurt to sit afterward? Did you bleed? More importantly, how was the orgasm? Dear lord, I bet it was amazing. Was it?"

Ella is beet red as she shakes her head. "I'm not talking about this now. Piper sent an SOS, and we still have no idea what happened, thanks to my husband's big-ass mouth. Now, Piper, tell us what's going on? Did Colin do something? Are we going to have to plot his death while we're there in a couple weeks?"

Kenzie cocks her head. "Murder is probably the only thing that would make me forget about anal. What do you need, girl?"

My heart feels so full, even though it's beating faster than the wings of a hummingbird. "First, I love you both, and you have no idea how much I am looking forward to your visit. Second, Colin didn't do anything wrong. Not really, anyway, but some of the events over the last twelve hours did have me telling him a secret that I should have told both of you a long time ago, and I couldn't wait any longer for you to know."

Ella's face softens, and she offers me a smile of encouragement. "Well, then. Tell us. What is it?"

I wait for Kenzie's smart-ass reply, but when it doesn't come, I take a steadying breath and finally let the words out. "I like writing. And not just random things, but books. Like the ones I edit. I have hundreds, maybe even thousands, of pages written that nobody has ever seen."

Kenzie rests her chin in her hand and flutters her eyes. "Please tell me they're naughty romance novels and then all is forgiven."

With a weight lifted off me, I grin. "Yes, there is a love story in them, but they're not smut. Sorry to disappoint."

She scoffs. "They're also not published yet. We can totally change that. You didn't convince me to start reading dirty novels only to tell me you won't write the same shit in yours. I won't stand for that. If you want my forgiveness for keeping this secret, then promise me you'll steam them up."

I laugh at her threat, mentally kicking my own ass for thinking this was going to be a bigger deal than it really is.

Though, it was a big deal to me and still is, so I'm not sure what is wrong or right here. All I do know is that I feel better telling them.

"Seriously, Pipe. This is amazing news, and I'm so proud of you for telling us something that makes you feel vulnerable, but what I really want to know is how did Colin find out?"

I blush, and Kenzie grins, but Ella cuts her off. "Don't you dare embarrass her into silence."

Kenzie pretends to zip her mouth closed and stays quiet.

"Well, he came over last night and brought whiskey, plus some card and board games to play. We ended up playing Never Have I Ever all night while drinking, and by the end, we were making up our own questions and I drunkenly told him. After that, he stayed the night and this morning he got up before me to make breakfast and happened to read some of what was up on my laptop."

Kenzie glares. "That British bastard snooped through your things?"

"Not really. At least, not how he explained it," I say before recounting the morning events. "He apologized for accidently invading my privacy and seemed super sincere. He could have not told me at all, so I don't think he was lying. Honestly, though, it's more of a relief to know I have no other dark secrets."

Ella raises a brow. "If you consider that dark, I don't want to know what you think about anal." We all laugh, and before the subject can be changed again, Ella then asks, "What did he think about your work?"

I can feel the flush covering my cheeks as I lean against the counter. "He said it was really great. That even after only reading a few paragraphs, I'd made him feel what the heroine was and that he wants to read more when I'm ready."

Kenzie rolls her eyes and sighs. "Of *course* it's fucking amazing. You're Piper Lucille Fitz. A badass. Even if you're only just learning that for yourself."

Tears prick in my eyes, and my lower lip trembles. "God, I miss you both so much." I can't stop the onslaught of crying that ensues after that.

My emotions are on a roller coaster I didn't sign up for. Any happiness I'd been feeling moments ago is overshadowed by the fact that I'd give anything to be having this conversation in person with them. I don't know how I'm supposed to live the rest of my life thousands of miles apart from my best friends. Kenzie and Ella are a part of me. My soul sisters.

"Hey." Ella's sharp tone sounds through my crying. "You better lift that phone back up so we can see your beautiful face and remind you again that everything is going to be okay. You're where you're supposed to be right now, and I feel that deep in my heart. I know it's hard to be apart, and more so for you because you've had to leave everything behind, but I promise you things are going to be okay. I just know it."

I wipe the tears and snot from my face. "I really want to believe you, and I'm trying to make the best of things here. It's just hard without you two."

Kenzie winks. "It's also hard with us and you know it. I agree with Ella, though. We'll be there soon, and I promise to drive you batshit crazy so that when it's time for us to go home, you'll be thankful. I'll have all the obnoxious things planned."

I snort-laugh through the last of my tears. "I don't think LA is ready for you, Kenzie Jane."

She straightens her shoulders proudly. "Probably not, but you're there so they have no choice. I'll be swinging in on my wrecking ball, causing all the mayhem I can. You know, without violating any relationship laws between me and Bentley, of course."

"I seriously can't wait," I say with a heavy sigh and back away from the kitchen counter to grab water that I badly need after a night of drinking.

After grabbing a bottle from the fridge, I head into the living room and sit on the couch with my phone still in hand. "I really like him, you guys. My freaking boss, who I'm not supposed to date."

Ella smiles and glances away from the phone briefly. "Sometimes the best things in life come when we're not ready for them, but that doesn't mean they aren't meant to be. If Colin is as great as you've made him sound, I can understand why you like him, but is what you feel enough to find a new job for or change departments? Assuming he has no intention of doing that instead."

I shrug. "We haven't really talked about that. We both agreed it was a problem for the future, but maybe it's time we got serious about that conversation. I've only been around him a month, and I don't think I can do much more without knowing where this is going long term."

"You could always just enjoy the sex and not care about where things are going," Kenzie says nonchalantly.

I bark out a laugh. "Ha! Like you did? Right. I know it

worked out well for you, but my situation is more complicated than yours was."

She shrugs. "It doesn't have to be if you don't let it."

I let her words sink in and wonder if my crazy best friend is right.

Doubtful this time, but maybe.

Chapter Twenty-Four

I HAVE AN IDEA

Colin

OVER A WEEK HAS PASSED SINCE THE NIGHT I stayed over at Piper's, and I'm pleased to share that there have been two other sleepovers. Both of them at my house, because...you guessed it, Sir Charles.

I haven't minded staying in. At least, not until a couple of days ago. I've been wanting to take her on a proper date for Valentine's Day, but Piper is too worried about anyone from work seeing us and asking questions that will either force us to lie or get us fired.

I understand her reasonings, but I think I've finally figured out a way around her hesitation, and I've worn my favorite green tie for good luck, hoping she won't tell me no.

I make my way down to her office. It's something I've done at least once a day to each of the six editors under me just so that I don't draw attention when I need to see Piper. My hands are in the pockets of my black slacks, and I left the suit jacket behind.

When I arrive, her door is cracked, and the blinds are actually closed. I stop and listen to make sure she's not on the phone, and all I can hear is the soft hum to some melody I feel like I should know but can't place.

I push forward and see Piper's glasses-covered eyes intently focused on her computer screen, her head bobbing, and a pencil pressed between her lips.

She doesn't see me enter, and I take in her thick leggings, purple skirt, and cream blouse. Her heels are on the floor just past the end of her desk, and she seems so relaxed.

I turn to leave, not wanting to interrupt her flow, but as I reach for the handle, Piper gasps. "Holy shit. How long have you been there?"

I'm smiling by the time I face her again. "Just a few seconds. When I realized how deep you were into the book, I didn't want to distract you."

She looks behind me and sees the door still mostly closed. "I couldn't focus earlier, so I blocked out as many distractions as I could."

My brow raises, and I tilt my head. "Why couldn't you focus?"

She cuts a hard glare my way. "I'm not answering that."

"That's answer enough, little bird." I laugh and step closer, but not too close in case anyone peeks in. "I have an idea. One that I want you to think about fully before you give me an answer. And try to keep an open mind."

Piper's teeth peek out, scraping over her lower lip. "Okay."

"So, with Valentine's Day in a couple days, I thought we could celebrate a day early to avoid the normal chaos. How does a road trip down to Long Beach sound? We could go see that new action movie together at the cinema and even check out the water, get some dinner, and watch the show before or after. It's an hour drive, and there should be no chance we'll see anyone we know."

By the time I'm done speaking, I can already see the denial in her eyes, so I plead with her a little more. "Just think about it and let me know by end of day. My idea will get us both out of work early tomorrow so we can go already knowing our other coworkers are here busy. Plus, everything should be pretty slow since it will be the day before the holiday."

She nods hesitantly and squeezes the arms of her chair. "Okay. I'll think about it, but only if you promise no gifts. I have secretly hated this day since I was a child."

I give her a smile and a wink for good measure. "Maybe you can tell me why tomorrow night during our long drive together."

She rolls her eyes at me and flicks her hand toward me. "Go away. I have work and apparently some thinking to do now."

Oh, she's so going to say yes.

———

By the next afternoon, everything has come together. Piper asked me if she could work from home for the rest of the day while I was in a meeting with Brian and Shannon, and I had already told everyone that morning that I had a potential client meeting and wouldn't be returning to the office when I left later in the day.

When I do, I meet Piper at her house, and before she can back out for the fifth time, we're headed down the 710 toward Long Beach. Even better, and almost as if this night is meant to be, traffic is clear, and the normally hour-long drive only takes forty minutes.

We decide to go see the movie first, so we aren't on any time constraints later, which sounded great to me until we were walking out of the theater.

I'm holding hands with Piper and beaming like a fool. "That was really amazing. Especially the battle at the end. I did not expect that guy to come out and destroy everything in his path."

She nods. "Agreed. That was the best part. I was thinking that maybe they could—"

Piper stops mid-sentence and shoves me into another screening room.

"What are—" I try to ask what she's doing, but her hand smacks over my face and she glares at me before glancing back out the door.

"Steve is here," she whispers, and I can now feel her entire body trembling.

I carefully remove her death grip on my face and check around the corner, but I don't see anything. "Steve, as in my boss?"

She rolls her eyes. "Do you think I'd care about any other Steve?"

"Valid point. What way did he go?" I ask, still unable to spot him.

Piper lets out a sigh. "I don't know. He was headed right toward us. I swear we made eye contact, but then I panicked and, well, you know the rest. Maybe he went into another movie already."

"I think if he saw us, he'd have come over here to out us, right?" I ask, hoping to calm her with my words and by grabbing her shaking hands.

Her wide eyes meet mine. "I don't know."

I tug her toward me and hold her tight, still staying in the shadows of the dim entrance to the screening room. "I'm sorry, Piper. I really thought this would be safe. If you'd rather go home instead of heading to dinner and the beach, I understand."

She shudders against me, and I hate myself so much right now. I shouldn't have risked things so soon. We were finally getting settled into a good place, and I have no idea how much this is going to set us back...or worse, destroy my chance at having a real relationship with this wonderful woman.

If Steve did see us and he asked me about why I was here with Piper, I'd quit. I wouldn't ruin her career when she isn't ready for anything else. I couldn't do that. But that doesn't mean she'd still keep me around. And that was what scared me most.

She nods against my chest. "Yeah, I think I'd like to go home now."

Fuck.

———

THE DRIVE HOME CONSISTED OF NEARLY NO conversation between Piper and me. She did some texting on her phone and stared out the window a lot. There was so much I wanted to say, yet nothing sounded good enough in my head to say out loud.

Instead, I stewed while she seemed to ponder a little too deeply.

When I dropped her off, I watched as her eyes scanned every person walking their dog down the street or out for a jog. She even checked the neighbors' yards to make sure nobody was outside.

And then, she barely kissed my cheek before darting for her door.

That night, I lay in bed for hours unable to sleep, yet I could think of no solution to make any of this better.

At least, that was the case until I finally fell asleep.

The dream I have is so vivid, just like the words it was inspired from. I watch helplessly as the woman runs from the beast, screaming for help, but there is nothing I can do.

When the silver wolf has her pinned beneath him, I think for sure I am about to witness her last breath, but then another wolf shows up, midnight in color and twice the size of the first wolf.

He plows the attacker over and the girl escapes, but I still don't know what becomes of her, because that's when I wake.

And now I know what I'm going to do to make everything okay.

At least, that's my hope...as long as nothing else blows up in my face.

Chapter Twenty-Five

A SHITTY THING

Piper

It's Friday, and for the last five or six Fridays, I've had an unspoken standing date with Colin. Yet, after the abrupt way our first official date ended, I'm just not sure I can pretend nothing has changed.

His boss, who really is both of ours, saw us the other night. There's no way he didn't. Though, the workday is almost over and I haven't seen Steve around in two days.

I'm not sure if that's a good thing or bad, but either way, it's a thing, one that is out of my control. I don't like not knowing what is going to happen.

Shannon knocks on my doorframe. "Happy Friyay! What are you doing tonight?"

I wish I could say having fantastic sex, but that's not happening.

"Not sure. What about you?" I ask, fidgeting with the paperclip on my desk. We have this same conversation nearly every Friday, and each time it gets harder to tell her

I'm busy. She probably thinks I'm lying, because I don't have any other friends here.

She smiles brightly, toying with a lock of blonde hair. "Well, I might have tickets to get into a club tonight where there's said to be a pop-up concert happening, but they're not saying who. Matt can't go and I thought I'd ask you."

My chest tightens, and a weight settles in my stomach. Shannon is my friend, and she clearly sees me as hers. Yet, she has no idea why I've been avoiding her outside of work.

I'm officially a terrible person.

In an attempt to fix that, I say, "I would love to go."

She leans against the door and tilts her head forward. "Seriously?"

I laugh, not at all offended. "I can say no if you'd rather."

She waves a hand back and forth in front of her. "Absolutely not. You're not getting out of this now. Do you want to meet me there or at your house? The club isn't too far from your place I don't think."

My fingers drum over the desk, and I grin. "My house. Then we'll call for a ride, so we don't have to worry about parking." Normally, I get a ride so I don't have to worry about drinking, but since Shannon is pregnant, I'll likely keep the alcohol to a minimum anyway.

She claps her hands and lets out a quick squeal. "Yes, I'm so excited! I was going to go by myself if you said no, and I'm so glad I can have my wingwoman to keep any unwanted people away from me while I'm just trying to enjoy some good music, you know?"

Did I know? Would I feel that way if someone hit on me tonight or asked me to dance and Shannon interfered? Would Colin be the reason I say no? Did this week really change anything for me? The fact that I'm not sure confuses the hell out of me.

———

Taylor mother-freaking-Swift. I nearly died when she stepped onto the stage. In none of our guessing had we considered her. Yet, there she'd been, singing and dancing along with everyone in the club as if she was just another person.

I mean, I realize she is, but still, I was starstruck and took a billion pictures and videos to remember the night by.

My arm wraps around Shannon as we make our way to a line of waiting cars. "Thank you for this. You have no idea how badly I needed it."

She rests her head against mine and squeezes my hand. "I'm glad you could join me. I was worried that new guy you're seeing would steal all of your attention and we'd never get to know each other outside of work."

"Yeah, I wouldn't worry too much about that," I say with a frown.

She gets distracted with finding us a car and my thoughts go dark for the first time all night. Colin hasn't texted or called since I told him I was busy tonight. I thought that would make me feel better, but instead, I feel like garbage and miss him.

I've had fun with Shannon and don't regret hanging out with her, but I wish my date with Colin had never happened and that I could be sharing the joy over my amazing night with him and not left wondering if Steve already talked to him without me knowing yet.

"This one is ours," Shannon says, tugging my hand until I'm following her into the back of a black sedan.

Once we're settled and have confirmed he has my address, Shannon shifts in her seat toward me. "So, that guy? He's not working out?"

I bite the inside of my cheek and shrug. "I don't know. It's just more complicated than I wanted things to be."

"You know when I first met Matt, we worked in the same department. Clearly, that was going to be an issue, but our meeting led me on a path I never saw for myself. Complicated doesn't always have to be bad if you don't want it to be. If you really like this guy, try to have a little faith that everything will work out if it's supposed to."

I hadn't known that about Matt and her. I only assumed one of them had joined the company after meeting, but I didn't want to change my career with Alliteration. There aren't any other positions there that I would consider taking.

I guess I could transfer genres and possibly end up at one of the other publishing houses they own around here, but I said yes to this one because they promised I could stick with what I loved most: fantasy.

Could I settle for something different while still doing what I enjoy and getting to be with Colin at the same time? Am I the only one of us wondering what they have to give up in order to make this work?

I don't think so. What I already know about Colin tells me he's not selfish like that, but I don't see any other options for us without asking him to likely take a step down from his current role. And that is something I'm equally not okay with.

Complicated might not always be a bad thing, but it sure is a shitty thing.

———

THE NEXT DAY, AND AFTER A VERBAL LASHING from Kenzie and Ella to stop being a chicken shit, I finally call Colin.

My hand shakes as I wait for him to answer, wondering if he even will. The phone keeps ringing, and I'm about to hang up when I hear a meow.

"Seriously, furball. Go away," Colin says from further away, then there's some rustling before I hear a deep "Hey."

"Everything okay over there?" I ask, fighting a smile even though he can't see me.

Colin sighs. "Yeah. Charlie was laying on my phone and I had the ringer off, so while I could hear the faint vibrating, I didn't realize it was being swallowed by his arse. And now I realize that sounds like I'm holding an arse phone to my ear and I'm kind of grossed out."

He gags, making me finally laugh. "I wasn't thinking that, but now that you've said something, the picture isn't great."

A few beats of silence later, he finally says, "Did you have fun with Shannon last night?"

My head leans back against the couch cushion, and I close my eyes. "I did. Taylor Swift showed up and sang a few of my favorite songs."

"No shit? I bet that was amazing. I'm glad you went." The excitement and sincerity in his voice hits me in the chest.

"Yeah, me too."

"Why doesn't it sound like you had fun?" he asks in a softer tone. I wish I could see him.

Reopening my eyes, I cross my ankles and sit up straighter. "I did, but that doesn't mean I haven't been stressing about other things."

His sigh is light, but I still hear it clearly. "I'm sorry,

Piper. I tried to talk to Steve, but I guess he's out of town for a week and I missed the email before we left that day. Last-minute family getaway. I haven't heard anything from him, but I promise you, if I do, I will make this right."

That is the problem Colin isn't understanding. I don't want him to make this right. I didn't want to be in the situation where someone had to give something up. It's not fair to either of us, and I finally say as much to him.

"I promised you before that I would figure something out and I meant it. Please trust me for now. I know that's a big ask, but I still think everything will be okay," he says with a conviction in his voice that I haven't heard before.

"I think I can do that, but I don't know for how long, Colin. This is getting harder by the week."

Even he can't deny that last part is true.

"Just a little bit longer. I promise." He pauses, and when he speaks again, I can hear the smile in his voice. "Aren't Kenzie and Ella going to be here in a few days?"

I laugh. "Good diversion. Don't think I don't see what you're doing, but yes, they'll be here Wednesday and leave on the following Monday."

"Since I don't want to bother you while they're here, do you think I could come see you today or tomorrow?" he asks, and the confidence he had moments before is gone.

I nod, even though he can't see me. "Yeah, I'd like that."

"Good. So would I."

After we make tentative plans for a time later, I lay on the couch and stare at the ceiling. I hope like hell I'm not letting myself get more attached to the sexy Brit only for us to be forced apart in the coming weeks.

That is the kind of heartbreak I'm not sure I can handle right now when I'm here, seemingly all on my own.

Chapter Twenty-Six

LITERALLY KILLING ME

Colin

WEDNESDAY HAS ARRIVED, AND I'M NOT SURE HOW I feel. I officially "met" Kenzie and Ella on a video chat this weekend with Piper, thinking that might be a good way to prepare for their arrival, but instead, I was met with smirking faces and very few words.

I absolutely didn't expect that.

Knowing they'll be here tonight and I'll meet them in person tomorrow, I'm at a loss on how I can attempt to be ready for whatever they're going to throw my way.

They're the two most important people in Piper's life. With how precarious things have been between us since last week, I know this has to go well. I can't be too pushy or aloof. I can't be too nice or rude. There's a balance somewhere that I have to find or everything I've been hoping for will never come to fruition.

I have my phone in hand and am sitting in bed. Piper should be back from the airport soon with her friends. I want to check and make sure they arrived okay, but I decide

209

to wait until I hear from her. She said she'd text, and I can have more patience.

With a groan, I run a hand through my already tousled hair. "It's like I'm a bloody teenager all over again."

Then, I freeze and glance at Charlie, who's snoring on the bed. If he didn't budge, maybe I was just hearing things, but I swore I heard laughter.

Sliding the covers back, I get out of bed and head for the living room. There's a woman peeking through my window, and she waves when our eyes meet.

"Oh hell," I mutter. I'm only wearing sweatpants, and it's too late to turn around. Kenzie is pointing to the door and twisting her hand as if to tell me I need to unlock the door.

Charlie finally makes his way out of the bedroom, whining loudly, but I ignore him and let the ladies in.

Piper is standing between Ella and Kenzie. She's not smiling, but she's not mad, either. I'm not sure how to read the situation.

"I tried to warn you, but that one stole my phone." Piper points to Ella, who wiggles her fingers at me.

"Hi, there. Are you going to invite us in?" she asks coyly.

I smile and nod. "Of course. Come on in. I'll just go put a shirt on."

Kenzie fans her face. "Shit. You weren't kidding. The accent is even more powerful in person." Then, she winks at me. "You really don't have to get dressed on our account."

I chuckle and smile at Piper who is now cringing with flushed cheeks. "Thanks, but I think I need to for myself."

Piper mouths an apology, but it's not needed.

"Well, go on then. We're just going to make ourselves at home," Kenzie adds when I take a step toward my room.

Ah, I understand now. This is a surprise visit to see how I am when I'm not expecting their company.

Well, I have nothing to hide. Kenzie can look around as much as her heart desires, but she's not going to find anything untoward.

When I walk out of my closet, she's peeking in my bedroom, and I raise a brow at her. "Can I help you?"

She grins, not at all ashamed of her snooping. "Nope. Thanks, though."

I watch as she enters and heads toward the bathroom, flicks on the lights for a few seconds, then comes back out, looks around my bed, then walks toward me.

She pats my shoulder. "You passed the first test, Colin Adamson. I'm impressed."

"Uh, thanks?" Piper said Kenzie had no filter, but I had assumed she exaggerated on *some* things. Now, I know better.

I follow Kenzie back down the hallway and find Ella poking through my cabinets. She looks at Kenzie and nods. "Clean here, too. No expired food or weird shit in the medicine cabinet."

Piper is sitting on the couch with her head between her hands. "You guys are killing me right now. Like literally killing me."

Kenzie jumps on the cushion next to her, then lays on top of Piper. "Oh, come on, Pipe. Did you really expect anything less when you told us you were fucking the handsome English man?"

"I'm going to die. Right here," Piper mutters into the couch. I decide to go and save her.

I pull on her hands, and she slides out from underneath Kenzie. My arm wraps around her waist, and I drag her toward me. "No dying tonight, and while I approve of your friends poking around, I don't approve of making my woman miserable." I meet Kenzie's and Ella's surprised gazes. "Can we be done with the torturing, at least for tonight?"

The two women share a look that tells me absolutely nothing while Piper hides against my chest.

Ella finally nods. "I think because you asked that can be arranged. For tonight."

Piper looks up at me, and I meet her gaze to finally see the joy I expected to find earlier. "Thank you. I owe you big for this," she whispers.

I kiss the top of her forehead. "No thanks necessary, but you could always send me some of those chapters I've been dying for."

She tenses in my hold, but not nearly as much as I expect before she shrugs. Interesting. This is the first time she hasn't told me no. While I haven't been pressuring her to share the work she's been so private with, I've made it clear I haven't lost interest. My hope is that it encourages her to keep writing.

Finally, we take a seat in the chair, and I position Piper in my lap. "How was the flight over?" I ask Kenzie and Ella.

Now, it's Ella who groans, then points at Kenzie. "That one told the pilot it was my first time on a plane and asked him if he wouldn't mind giving me a tour of his *cock*pit."

Air gets stuck in my throat. "Aren't you married?"

She nods. "And happily so."

Kenzie shoves her shoulder into Ella's. "I could have slipped you another dildo. You should be thankful my antics have calmed down some."

Ella glares, and Piper giggles in my lap. "Do I even want to know?" I ask her.

She nods. "But I'll tell you later."

And that's how the next hour goes. The three women bantering back and forth like no time has passed since they parted, and the stories? They are something else entirely. I find myself wondering about the men Owen and Bentley that they keep mentioning. Those poor blokes have been through some shit with these ladies.

Except even hearing all the crazy, I can't help but hope my future will be filled with the same insane stories.

———

THE NEXT MORNING, PIPER ISN'T AT WORK, BUT when I log into my email, I see something from her that she sent just twenty minutes before. The message is titled "Thank you", and I quickly open it to find an attachment with a very short message.

I'm sorry about last night. To show my appreciation of you not kicking us out, here are the first three chapters. No promises when you'll get more.
Piper

Without waiting a second longer, I download the Word file and open it to see twenty-one pages included. I have so many other things I'm supposed to be doing right now, but instead of worrying about that, I devour every sentence Piper has sent me.

Before I know it, the mouse won't scroll down any further and I've reached the end. The grin on my face is beginning to ache and I'm tempted to start reading everything all over again, but before I can, a shadow casts over my desk.

I look up to find Steve staring down at me. "Good morning, Colin."

His voice is missing the normally jovial tone I'm used to hearing from him, but I try to keep the worry out of my own.

"Good morning indeed," I reply. "How was your holiday?"

He glances at my screen then back at my face. "Fine. Do you have time to meet this morning?"

I don't really, but considering the way he's acting, and knowing Piper saw him at the movies, I know I have no other choice but to say yes.

"Sure, I can be there within a half hour if that works for you," I say, forcing a smile to my face.

His lips thin. "Now would be better."

Shit. I'm not ready to talk with him if he's going to bring up Piper.

I had a plan, and it isn't ready yet because I haven't gotten her permission, and that thirty minutes I asked for really could have helped me improvise. With the way Steve is still staring down on me, though, I don't bother further pissing him off.

"Sure." I lock my computer screen and push away from my desk before following him to his office.

I had hoped since Steve didn't say anything before now about seeing me with Piper that he was maybe going to pretend he didn't. If that had been the case, my plan was to convince Piper to give me her chapters, tell her how much I loved them, and convince her to let me show Steve.

I knew that would take time, so it was a gamble to begin with, but if we'd been careful moving forward, I thought it might work.

As I walk silently behind Steve, I'm scrambling to find

the words I can use to keep from getting myself and Piper fired right now, but nothing is coming to me.

When I take a seat in the office, my heart is beating wildly, and my palms are damp. Damn it. Why couldn't he have waited a little longer to bring this up? I had the chapters now. I was getting so close to having everything come together.

Steve is staring at me with a raised brow. "Is everything okay, Colin?"

I nod and pull at the collar of my shirt that suddenly feels too tight. "Yep. What did you want to talk about?"

"Several things, actually." He leans back in his chair and steeples his fingers. "I don't know if you heard or not, but we were able to make a couple deals from those chapters your team read. The Benton one might even already have screenwriters looking at it."

"That's great. I'm glad we were able to help," I say while my chest loosens a bit. Maybe he isn't going to bring up Piper...

He nods. "Me, too. I also heard there was an issue with the Pearson file while I was gone, but you stepped in and found a solution that worked for the author and Alliteration. Well done, again."

"I'm just happy we didn't have to bother you while you were away." I swallow hard and press my palms over my thighs.

Steve lets out a slow and heavy sigh before leaning forward to rest his forearms against his desk. "Listen, I hate to be having this conversation, but I can't avoid what needs to be said, no matter how much I wish I could."

Bloody hell. I'm fucked.

"I saw something I can't unsee, Colin, something that could cost me my job if I don't say anything but could also cost me one of the best editor-in-chiefs this company has ever had."

Any hope I'd had that Steve might not say anything is quickly dashed away. Even worse, he's had time to think about what he's going to do about it.

I sit up straighter and try to remain sure of my words. "Listen, I can explain."

He waves a hand, cutting me off. "No need. I know what I saw, Colin. You're dating Piper. Something both of you know goes against the contracts you signed."

"I know, but—"

"I'm not done. We have solutions, and I've spent some time listening to the advice of my wiser half. Did you know my Sarah used to work here? That she was my boss when I first started with Alliteration?"

I give my head a slight shake. "I didn't."

His eyes shine under the fluorescent lights. "She stole my breath the first time I saw her. Back then, the no dating clause wasn't a thing, but still, Sarah had worked hard to get where she was and wanted things to be kept quiet. That choice nearly ruined us, but we persevered, and twenty-two years later, we're still going strong."

"That's great to hear. I'm happy for the two of you." My words feel forced, and I have no clue where Steve is going with all this, but it would be great if he'd get to the point.

"She's still my sounding board." He clasps his hands together. "She even talked me out of firing both you and Piper."

The gulp that travels down my throat burns with severity. "Please pass along my thanks."

Steve chuckles. "I can do that, and I can also pretend I

didn't see what I saw if you can promise me that it was a one-time thing."

I'm tempted to lie to him and say that's the case, but I can't. It's not the right way for Piper and me to find a solution to our problem. Neither is what I'm about to do, but I hope she'll forgive me for deviating from my plans and understand I had no other choice.

"My date with Piper wasn't a one-time thing, nor do I intend to stop seeing her." Damn, it feels good to say that out loud.

Steve raises a brow. "So, then one of you is transferring departments or quitting? That's the only choice left unless you're going to force me to fire you both."

That's the last thing I want, and I say as much. "But I do have another option. One I'm not quite prepared to present. If you could give me some more time, I think you'll be pleased with my proposal."

I'd yet to see anything make Steve happier than landing a new book deal. Hopefully, he's feeling patient today.

"You're a good employee, Colin. I wish I hadn't seen what I did, but I did. I can't give you any more time. You can either tell me what this 'proposal' of yours is or I'll do what needs to be done. I know that's harsh, but I can't bend the rules for one set of employees without having a lawsuit from others on my hands. I have to put Alliteration first here."

Shit. I know what he's saying makes sense. I understand his position, but...fuck. Piper better forgive me for this.

"Piper is writing a story, one that I strongly believe will interest you. She's not quite ready to share it, which is why I was hoping for more time, but I do have the first three chapters and they're solid. If you could reconsider, I promise that nobody will see us together again until

Alliteration is no longer an issue for us." As I say the words out loud, my stomach churns.

This is a terrible idea, but I don't know what else to do.

"Are you saying you believe I'll want to make Piper a publishing deal, and then your problems will be solved because she'll no longer work here?" Steve asks, a little less pissed than he was moments ago.

I nod. "That's my hope, but I need more time to pull everything together."

He drums his fingers over the desk. "And what if she doesn't want what I have to offer?"

"Then, I guess I'll be able to tell you that I'm no longer dating my employee, but it's a risk I believe worth taking."

Steve leans back in his chair and shakes his head, but there's a smile playing on his lips. "I'm not going to make you promises, but you can have a little more time, only if you give me those chapters. I need proof that the risk I'm taking is worth the potential reward."

It's one thing to tell Steve about Piper's writing, but to share the chapters she's only just given me? I don't know that I can do that, but I attempt to procrastinate a little more.

"Sure. I can send those over as soon as she's back at work. Her friends are in town and she's taking some time off."

He shakes his head. "Today, Colin. No later or I'll know what I need to do."

"Okay. Today. Got it."

Fuck. I don't know if I just saved everything from falling apart or ruined everything.

Chapter Twenty-Seven

BRITISH DICK

Piper

HAVING ELLA AND KENZIE AT MY HOUSE IS THE best feeling ever. I only have them for five days, but I plan to cherish each minute I get to spend with them.

Colin said I could work from home while they're here and even take some half days, so I'm taking advantage of that today.

The first thing I'd done when I logged on this morning was send him a thank-you in the form of my first three chapters. I nearly vomited as I hit send, but the more people that know about my writing, the more excited I get about it.

I'd thought it would take me months to move past the fear of letting others see and judge my words, but it's only been weeks now and I can't wait to hear what Colin thinks. Sure, he could lie to me, but I don't think he will. At least, I hope not.

Even more, I hope I'll be the kind of author who can take constructive criticism without losing her cool.

Oh, God. I just called myself an author. Nope. Too much, too soon. I'm still just a writer.

I'm going to blame that errant thought on the fact that I didn't get much sleep last night. We were up late after getting back to my place once they were done interrogating Colin. Ella and Kenzie are still sleeping while I work in my bed from my laptop.

Just as I'm finishing up a chapter, Ella shuffles past my bedroom door. "I somehow forgot what overdrinking is like when it's the three of us together. I'm getting too old for this shit."

I laugh and close my laptop before sliding off the mattress. "Go take a hot shower and I'll get coffee ready."

She nods and continues stumbling toward the bathroom. I make my way downstairs, smiling as I skip down the steps. I have missed them so damn much that I'm pretty sure my heart might explode at some point while they're here.

I get the coffee going and start digging through the cabinets for the breakfast goodies I bought yesterday. When I turn around with my arms full of donuts, pastries, and fruit to cut, Kenzie nearly gives me a heart attack.

She's standing next to the counter with crazy hair and death in her eyes. "You better appreciate how much I love you, because this is the first morning I've woken up without a dick poking me in the ass in a long time. I don't like it."

I choke on air as I attempt to laugh at her craziness. "I bet we could convince Ella to wear a strap-on and spoon you."

She smirks and slides onto the stool. "If you mean blackmail when you say 'convince', then I would have to agree." Kenzie's palm slaps on the counter. "Now, feed me, wench. I require sustenance before I can do anything since I didn't get my morning D."

The box of donuts thuds against her hand when I push it across the counter. "Enjoy."

She pulls out a cream-filled, maple-glazed long john, then takes a huge bite of it while moaning. "Creamy. Just how I like it."

Ella strolls into the kitchen. "I see we're already on to dirty talk. Good to know." She snags a cinnamon twist and reaches for a napkin before leaning against the counter. "So, what's the plan today?"

I'm cutting up apples while I answer. "I was thinking we could head over to Hollywood and do some tourist things today if you're both up for it."

Ella nods and speaks with sugar coating her lips from the donut. "We should hike to the Hollywood sign while we're there."

"Absolutely," I say just as Kenzie mutters, "Fuck you."

Ella gives her a soft shove. "Come on. There's a walking path and it will be painless. I promise."

"That's what you said about the waterfall 'walk' from hell," Kenzie snarls, wiping cream filling from her chin.

Ella pulls her phone from her pocket and starts typing before handing it over to Kenzie. "Look. Even old people can handle it. You'll be fine."

Kenzie glares and gets up. "Alive and fine are two totally different things. I'm taking a shower now." Then she snags the first cup of coffee. "And taking this with me. Maybe I won't hate the both of you so much when I return."

Ella and I watch her stomp toward the stairs, and then laughter bursts from both of us once she's out of sight.

"Bitches!" Kenzie yells and causes our amusement to spike all over again.

Ella's arms wrap around me. "This is the best. We need to somehow make this happen every month. Waiting two months to see you isn't okay with me."

My chest constricts, but I can't find the words to respond. Not because I don't agree with her, but because the ache I feel without them is just too damn strong.

Ella pops an apple slice into her mouth, then takes a seat, seeming to realize that is a conversation I'm not ready for yet.

"So, Colin. I like him," she adds when I finish cutting the fruit.

My cheeks heat and lift. "I do, too."

"You wouldn't say," she teases. "Have you decided what you're going to do about the work situation?"

I groan and start cleaning up. "No, and not because I haven't thought about it, but there's nothing we can do unless one of us decides to work for another department. I hate to sound selfish, but I didn't leave everything I love to do something I don't enjoy like marketing or accounting or editing books I don't appreciate. And I'm sure Colin feels the same way, considering he moved from London to take this job."

Ella's lips purse together. "You're at an impasse."

"So it seems," I say with a sigh before grabbing a pastry.

"You know you're going to have to choose at some point. Possibly before you're ready, but the sooner you do, the better off your heart will be. You can't keep this up without falling in love with that man. I saw the way he looks at you. You're probably already a goner, which I'm sure makes this worse, but don't prolong the inevitable, Pipe. I want the best for you, so I'll support whatever you decide. Just do it soon."

I hate how right she is. I hate even more that I want to

choose Colin over my work, but what scares me most is that if I do and things don't work out, I'll have thrown away my career for a man. I don't know that I can stomach that.

"You want to hear a secret before Kenzie?" Ella asks with a bright smile on her face.

My eyes immediately cast to her stomach. "Are you pregnant?"

Her eyes roll hard. "Of course not. Do you think I would have drank with you two last night if I was?"

I palm my forehead. "Duh. Sorry. What is it?"

She glances around and lowers her voice. "I might be soon, though."

I smile so big that my cheeks hurt, and I walk around the counter to hug her tight. "I'm so happy for you, El. You're going to make an excellent mother."

She nods against my shoulder. "We're going to start trying when I get back. I wanted to enjoy this trip first, but I stopped my birth control yesterday." She pulls back and there are tears of joy in her eyes. "I can't wait to call you Auntie Piper!"

An ache instantly slams into me, and I can't fight back the tears any longer. "Your baby won't even know me."

Ella shushes me and pulls me back tightly into her arms. "Yes, they will. No matter what, even if it's not the conventional way, you'll always be part of my family. Don't you ever think otherwise."

I try to accept her response, but there's a hole growing bigger inside me, one so large that I'm no longer sure about any of the decisions I've made over the last few months.

Kenzie joins us and throws her arms around our shoulders. "What did I miss?"

We pull apart, and I wipe the tears from my cheeks as

Ella answers, "Owen and I are going to start trying for a baby once we get back to North Carolina."

Kenzie groans and glares at Ella. "Damn it, woman. I am not motherly material, and you know Owen is going to convince Bentley that we need to get on this baby train. You can't wait a while longer?"

Ella rolls her eyes and smiles. "Sorry. Not happening. You'll have to find a way to say no to your fiancé."

"Or find a way to silence your husband." Kenzie rubs her hands together, and there's a glint of something evil in her green eyes.

"How does Hollywood sound to everyone now?" I ask, changing the subject, half because Kenzie shouldn't be allowed time to plot against Owen and half because I can't handle the emotional conversation anymore.

"Yeah, as long as I get my picture taken with a hot celeb downtown, then I guess I'll go," Kenzie answers as she refills her coffee cup.

Ella heads for the stairs. "I just need to grab my tennis shoes."

Kenzie quietly drinks her coffee, and I grab my bag from the couch to toss some snacks and waters inside. Even if we're not really hiking, I know better than to be gone for the day without something to keep Kenzie from whining.

———

TOO MANY HOURS LATER, WE FINALLY MAKE IT TO the top of the trailhead for the Hollywood sign. Ella is ready to strangle Kenzie, and Kenzie has threatened my life more times than I care to count.

And we're officially out of snacks.

"Tomorrow, we're spending all day at the beach. I don't

care if you bitches don't agree. That's what we're doing," Kenzie heaves as she leans against a wooden fence.

I walk over to her and lean my head against her shoulder. "Deal. But look out in front of you. Where else can you find views like this?"

"The internet," she grumbles, making me laugh.

Ella is at least enjoying herself. Or so it seems as I watch her snap a few photos, then take a video before joining us at the fence. "This is pretty awesome."

I nod in agreement. "Even better because we're all together."

Kenzie sighs. "I want to disagree with that, but I really can't."

"Good because we need to take some pictures of the three of us, and I won't put any of them on the wall if you're glaring in every one," I say, only mildly joking.

Kenzie takes Ella's phone. "My arms are longer. Let me take it."

We take a few good ones, then some goofy ones, and some just of each of us so that they're not all selfies. By the time we're done, my stomach is growling and I'm ready to head back, but I don't say anything because the views really are inspirational.

I think about Colin and work and my friends and hell, even my book. Colin thanked me via text for the chapters, but he didn't say whether he'd read them or not. I almost asked him when he'd read them, but I'm okay with being surprised. I wouldn't have thought that would be the case.

Ella nudges me. "What are you smiling for?"

"I was just thinking about the book I've been working on," I answer and embrace the flutters in my stomach instead of dreading them.

Kenzie leans forward and waggles her brows at me. "Is there dirty sex in it yet?"

My eyes roll, and I shake my head even though I'm smiling. "No, but there's romance as I already told you. The main character gets saved by an alpha wolf shifter and learns she's his fated mate."

Kenzie's eyes glaze over. "Fated what?"

"Soulmate in paranormal romance terms," I answer with a chuckle. "I didn't do sex on the page so all ages could read it."

Ella's mouth pops open and she grabs my forearm. "Does that mean you're going to publish it?"

Her shock isn't one-sided. I can't even believe I said those words. "I don't know. I guess I just wanted the option. I sent Colin the first few chapters this morning as a thank you for putting up with the two of you last night."

Ella scoffs. "Rude. I was an angel, but also not fair. I want to read them, too. And more than Colin got. He can't get everything first just because you're sleeping with him."

"Fine. Just don't tell me what you think. Not even good stuff. I won't believe you anyway. And just remember, it's not done." Okay, maybe now I'm nervous. I should have only agreed to the three chapters like I sent Colin.

Kenzie laughs. "Easy there, Pipe. Nobody wants to see what you ate for lunch earlier."

"Yeah, neither do I," I groan.

They both hug me, and Ella says, "It's going to be okay. There's no need to be nervous. I already know I'm going to love it and will be demanding the end from you when I get through whatever you send me."

"We'll see. I've yet to finish a full book. Just because I've been working on this one more, doesn't mean I'll be able to write the ending it deserves. I could lose my motivation at any point. Hell, you might not even want to read what I have because of that and that would be okay."

That's a lie. It would be great if Ella just didn't want to read any part of the book.

Ella gives me a smile I don't like. "I think thanks to the new man in your life, you're going to have all the motivation you need to finish. I'm not worried about a thing."

"Or, more specifically, his British dick is the influencer," Kenzie adds, oh-so tactfully.

This time, I don't even bother to refute their statements.

"Maybe it is."

Chapter Twenty-Eight

DESSERT BEFORE DINNER

Colin

AFTER MY MEETING WITH STEVE, I TRIED NOT TO let my day be ruined, but without Piper here to give me a reason to smile, staying positive was hard. It wasn't until she sent me a picture of her in front of the Hollywood sign, plus a selfie of all three of them, that my day was brightened.

I wanted to tell her about what I'd done, but I didn't want to ruin the fun she's having with Ella and Kenzie. Before leaving work, I regretfully sent the chapters to Steve after having read them several times myself.

I asked him for a week, but he hasn't responded yet. My hope is that the longer he takes to respond, the more time I'll have, but I force those thoughts from my mind and ready myself for a night with Piper and her friends.

As soon as I know they are on their way back, I volunteer to bring pizza over. After stopping by the store to pick up drinks as well, I grab the food and pull up to Piper's only a couple minutes before they do.

"I fucking hate you both," Kenzie says before slamming the passenger door and turning her back on the car. "You're lucky this isn't my house, or I'd lock you bitches out."

Piper gets out from behind the wheel, and Ella exits the back seat on Piper's side. Both of them are covering their mouths, trying and obviously failing to stifle their laughter.

"Oh, come on, Kenz. You know I didn't mean to," Piper says, then waves at me as I approach with pizzas in one hand and a bag of drinks in the other.

"Food," Ella practically growls before taking the two extra-large boxes from my hand.

Kenzie's head whips around. "Food? What kind of food?"

"Pizza. Plus, I brought wine and beer," I answer, adjusting my hold on the heavy bag.

Kenzie points at me. "You, I like. These other two? Don't trust them further than you can throw them."

Kenzie follows Ella to the front door, and I tilt my head at Piper. "Do I want to know what happened?"

"Kenzie's shoe was untied, and I might have stepped on the laces, which might have caused her to go tumbling down the trail while also ripping her pants, showing everyone around us that she was in fact not wearing underwear," Piper says, and her smile grows bigger the longer she talks.

I lean forward and give her a quick kiss. "Sounds like I missed one hell of a hike."

Kenzie pounds on the still-closed door. "You better unlock this stupid thing before I kick it in."

Piper sighs and pulls keys from her purse. "I'm coming."

Kenzie grunts. "You better not be."

Even I can't stop the snort of laughter that escapes me,

which causes Piper to cover her face. "Do you want me to leave the drinks and head home?" I ask her.

Ella pokes me in the chest. "Don't think you're getting out of here so easily, mister. If you're dating our girl, you're dating all three of us. We're going to have some quality family time tonight."

I swallow hard at that. With how feisty they seem, I'm not sure this is going to be good for me, but I do my best not to show my fear, afraid that will only fuel the interrogations I assume are coming.

Piper opens the door, and Kenzie storms ahead. Her left arse cheek is on full display, and there's a massive bruise forming there that looks bloody painful. I avert my eyes and understand why she's angry.

While Kenzie goes up to change, the rest of us head for the kitchen. I grab paper plates then glasses for everyone.

Ella raises a brow. "You seem to know your way around this kitchen pretty well, Colin."

I glance at Piper, and she just shrugs. Apparently, I'm on my own here.

"I suppose so." I pull out the two cases of beer and the wine bottles. "What's your beverage choice?"

She points to the wine. "White, please."

I get to pouring two glasses and hand one to each Ella and Piper at the same time.

"So, Colin. Were there no publishing companies that would hire you across the pond?" she asks after finishing a bite of pizza.

I choke a little on the beer I just opened. "No, I quite enjoyed my work there. I'd actually turned Alliteration down on a few occasions over the last several years. My mum was sick for a while, and I couldn't leave her alone after my brother moved to Scotland."

Ella downs half her glass in one go, then asks, "But you could now?"

Piper shoves Ella's arm. "She passed away. Maybe ease up a bit."

I offer Piper a small smile. "It's okay. She's only looking out for her friend."

"Best friend. Hell, my family, if we want to get specific," Ella says, then adds, "but I am sorry about your mother."

I nod and get my own pizza. "Thank you."

Kenzie's stomping can be heard coming downstairs, and I brace myself for more crazy, but she doesn't say much as she walks into the kitchen, hair bundled high up on her head, and grabs a plate. "Thanks for the food, Colin."

"Um, you're welcome. There's beer and wine as well," I say, pointing to the bottles as if she can't see them right next to her.

"Red, please." Kenzie hops up onto the counter and winces as she gets settled.

I meet Piper's gaze, but she merely shrugs. I may not know her friends well, but even I'm confused with Kenzie's mood.

Still, I pour the drink and hand it over.

"Thank you again." She takes a sip, then adds, "Will you tell your girlfriend and her friend that I'm not talking to them anymore after seeing the purple monster growing on my ass?"

"Sure. I can pass that along," I say before turning to Piper, who is rolling her eyes.

"Oh, come on, Kenz. It's not like I intentionally set out to hurt you. It was an accident, one that happened to be incredibly entertaining. You getting hurt is just an unfortunate part of it."

Kenzie picks a pepperoni from her pizza and throws it.

The greasy topping lands in the middle of Piper's forehead with an audible slap, and Piper squeals. "Holy hell, that's hot."

When she removes the pepperoni from her skin, there's a red circle on her skin and Kenzie chuckles. "Serves you right."

"I have to pee. Don't do anything funny while I'm gone," Ella says and moves to walk away, then turns back and grabs her plate and drink before pointing at all three of us. "I don't trust any of you."

When she disappears, I say, "I can see how Ella doesn't trust the two of you, but how did I get thrown in that mix?"

Kenzie grins, then nods at Piper. "You put your dick in that one."

Piper chokes on the wine she's drinking and sputters, dribbling liquid down the front of her shirt. "Damn it. I'm going to change and put this in the laundry."

Before I can object, I'm left alone with Kenzie. I glance back at the hallway, wondering if Ella is almost done, then feel a heel in my spine.

"So, Colin. What are your intentions with our Piper?" she asks hauntingly.

I cough a little and step back so she can't kick me again. "Intentions?"

Kenzie nods and sighs. "Yes. As in, what are your plans with this work issue we've heard about? Because if you don't have a plan and Piper gets hurt, I will come for you, and you won't ever be able to get me out of your nightmares."

I'd love to tell her that I have a great plan, but since that just recently got screwed up, I flounder for words. "Whatever happens, I won't let Piper get hurt."

She pats my shoulder as if I'm a child. "That's cute you seem to believe you have any control over that, but seriously... What's your plan?"

"Colin, can you come up here," Piper yells from the stairs. "I got a weird email from work."

I gladly take another step away from Kenzie. "Be right there."

She reaches for me, but misses, then I nearly run Ella over in my haste to keep Kenzie from trying to keep me in the kitchen again.

Kenzie's echoing laugh follows me upstairs. "You can run, but you can't hide, Colin Adamson!"

My shoulders shudder. I'm sure as hell going to try.

When I get to Piper's room, she's standing at the edge of her bed, frowning at her phone. She turns it toward me. "Do you know what this means?"

My stomach churns, hoping Steve hasn't said anything to her. When I skim over the email, I see it's to our whole department about changes coming that will impact the company as a whole.

"Oh, this is just about the integration of the smaller publishing houses. It seems they're wanting people to know there may be job opportunities in other states once everything is done," I answer as the knot in my chest loosens ever so slightly.

Piper nods and walks toward her closet, removing her shirt as she goes. Then with her back still to me, she takes off the sports bra. "Ugh, now that I took that off, I can smell myself. I'm going to take a shower."

My eyes watch her carefully, and I know I shouldn't, but damn, I want her. Right now. Regardless of anyone being downstairs.

She reaches for a new shirt, then bends over to get

something out of her dresser, but my eyes don't leave her arse in those skin-tight leggings.

When she turns around, I'm nearly within touching distance.

"Colin," she warns.

"Yes, little bird."

She glances at the still open door. "Kenzie and Ella are here. Did you forget?"

"Nope." I kick my foot out, and the door clicks closed.

Her body trembles before me. "They'll know what we're doing up here."

I chuckle. "Your friends were already talking about my dick. I don't think it can get much worse."

She tilts her head and, before I can capture her mouth, she says, "It really can."

"I'm up for the challenge." My lips press against hers, then I back up just an inch. "Unless you're not, then I'll head back down."

Piper's mouth twitches, and she grabs my shirt before dragging me to the bathroom. "Not a chance in hell."

She turns on the shower, and I strip out of my clothes faster than ever before. I reach into the top drawer and grab a condom while Piper gets naked. As soon as we're both ready, I grab her waist and lift her onto the counter.

"No shower sex?" she asks with a grin.

"The water better serves as a means to drown out your screams," I answer as I spread her legs and run my fingers over her wet slit.

A rumble builds in my chest, and I don't waste any time before I push up onto my toes, allowing my dick to settle inside her slick heat.

"Fuck, you feel so damn good," I growl into her ear,

thrusting harder until her nails are digging into my shoulders.

She uses her hands to keep herself propped up, and her ass is barely touching the counter now as she rides me harder, no longer sensitive to the size of my cock.

Her moans increase, and I capture her mouth, hoping to quiet the sound. Her friends might figure out what we're doing up here, but they don't need any more ammunition to taunt us with than they'll already have.

My tongue sweeps inside her mouth, and her cries echo inside the bathroom, regardless of my effort. "Holy hell, don't stop," she begs.

I don't intend to, but this isn't going to last long, either. My fingers tangle with her hair, and I grip the long strands tightly, pulling taut so I can see her face.

Her eyes are closed, and she's biting her lip while making delicious mewling noises that have my speed increasing.

"Look at me, little bird. Watch me while you come undone," I demand, feeling my balls tighten and knowing I'm not far behind her.

Piper's eyes flutter open and lock on to me. One of my hands moves up her side and cups her breast while my fingers pinch her nipple hard.

She gasps, the sound encouraging my movements to quicken. Her pussy tightens almost painfully around my dick, and I'm pretty sure I'm going to have bruises, or possibly gouges, where her nails are digging into my skin.

"So close," she mutters, still keeping her gaze on mine.

Her hips roll under my hold, and she rubs her clit against me while I'm still rocking back and forth inside her.

"Oh, God," she cries and presses her forehead against mine while tremors shatter her body within my hands.

I thrust harder, giving her all that I have and find my release as she's still coming down from her own high.

Her pussy clenches around my dick through the last of her aftershocks, and she lets out a shuddering breath before smiling widely. "We're never going to hear the end of this."

I brush her hair behind her ear. "Only because they're jealous."

"Ha, probably," she says, wiggling to try to get back onto her feet, but I don't release her.

Instead, I wrap my arms around her and hold her tight against me, wanting to say so much in that moment, but knowing I should wait until we're truly alone.

When I finally pull back, Piper looks up at me. "Are you okay?"

I nod and grin. "Better than I have been since the last time we had sex."

She gives me a light shove. "Get out of here so I can shower."

I grab a washcloth to clean myself up and do as she asks, but before I can leave the bathroom, she calls my name.

When I turn around, I see a smile on her face that's never been bigger. "Good luck out there."

"I can handle them. Take your time." As I'm closing the door, I hope like hell I don't soon regret those words.

Quickly, I give myself a wipe down and get dressed again. Then, I head downstairs to face the firing squad with a grin on my face.

Kenzie and Ella have moved from the kitchen to the living room. Their eyes are on me as I walk past them and toward the kitchen. I never did get to have my pizza.

I grab my beer and a few slices of pepperoni, then go sit on the couch next to Ella.

They're still silent. Just as I wonder who's going to break first, Kenzie opens her mouth.

"I don't know how they do things in London, but you're not supposed to get your dessert before dinner here," she says with a raised brow.

I swallow my bite and pretend to ponder her words. "Huh. Piper sure hasn't been complaining."

Ella snickers and Kenzie glares, seemingly disappointed she didn't rile me with her frankness.

"Maybe it just doesn't last long enough to feel like dessert for her," Kenzie adds.

I give her a feigned smile. "Or maybe I'm just so good at 'dessert' that she doesn't need it to last for hours every time. Would you like me to have a chat with Bentley for you?"

Ella's laughter echoes around us, and Kenzie merely smirks. "Touché, Adamson. Touché. You're going to fit right in with us."

"Fit in? He's going to be the second-best thing that ever happened to Piper," Ella says, and I don't bother to ask what the first is.

Chapter Twenty-Nine

SOUL SISTERS

Piper

MY TIME WITH ELLA AND KENZIE IS OVER, AND I
don't know how to say goodbye. Not when I know Ella is
going to be trying for a baby and Kenzie will likely be
planning a wedding with Bentley sooner rather than later.
My heart feels like it's being shattered all over again.
Possibly even worse this time.

Tears track down each of our cheeks as we hug outside
the airport security. "I want to be getting on that plane with
you," I murmur between them.

"I can shove you in my carry-on if you're feeling
flexible," Kenzie offers as she swipes at her face.

Ella squeezes my hand as we all pull apart. "It's going to
be okay. You'll be out for Easter next month and we'll figure
the summer out while you're there."

I nod and try to smile, but the action just doesn't
happen.

"At least you have Colin, and we know you're not all
alone here," Kenzie says. "We like him, Pipe. Like, really do.

I hope the two of you can figure out a way to make this all work."

God, I hope so, because the need to quit my job and go home to North Carolina is stronger right now than it's been at any point over the last two months.

"I'll let you know when we do," I reply and wrap my arms around both of them again. "I don't think I can let you go."

The tears start anew, and my chest burns with agony. I can't release them and watch them disappear through security. I need them too damn much.

Ella grabs my face with both of her hands and stares intently at me. "Everything is going to be okay. I promise. We're going to go, but it's not forever. We'll hug you again in four weeks, and we'll see you just as soon as we land."

Seeing through video chat isn't the same as seeing them like I am now, but I didn't need to tell Ella that. She knows it and I get that she's only trying to make me feel better.

My eyes move between the two of them. "I love you, but I'm going to go first. I don't think I can watch you walk away."

Kenzie hugs me one last time. "You're the bravest person I know. Remember that, no matter what happens next."

Kenzie saying nice things to me isn't helping. I just need to leave, because prolonging the goodbye is only making me cry more.

Ella blows me a kiss. "We love you. Drive carefully."

I nod and quickly turn around. When I get to the exit, I glance back to find them still standing there and waving at me.

Damn it. Why did I have to have the best friends in the world? Why did they have to make me miss them so much?

I take a shaky inhale, then wave once more before practically running to my car. When I get there, I let myself wallow in the hot tears trailing down my face for a few minutes.

As I start my car, I know there's only one other person who might be able to soothe the aches I'm being assaulted with, and I point my tires in his direction without thinking twice.

———

When I get to Colin's, the garage is already open for me, and I park beside his car. The tears have stopped falling, but the hollowness inside me is still there, as if someone is having a grand time carving my chest out with a spoon.

The door opens and Colin steps out, arms open. I fall into them willingly and start to cry all over again.

His hands move comfortingly over my back, and he whispers sweet words in my ear that I can barely process through my own misery.

I know Kenzie and Ella aren't dead, but the agony inside me says the distance between us is nearly the same.

Dramatic? Sure, but I don't care. Those two women are my soul sisters, and I don't know how I ever thought I could survive being apart from them.

Colin leads me inside and guides me to the couch, where it seems like he was working since his laptop is out. "I'm going to get you some tea and be right back. A good cuppa makes everything better."

I nod robotically, unable to reply verbally or look to see his face, even though I know he's only trying to cheer me up.

His footfalls sound through the otherwise quiet room, and then I hear the sweetest sound coming from behind me.

Sir Charles is on the back of the couch, and his green eyes are staring at me with all the love the feline can offer.

I reach for him and snuggle him to my chest. His head pushes against my chin, and my shoulders shake all over again. Maybe I need my own cat to keep me company in my lonely house.

Colin returns with the tea, but I don't reach for the cup. Instead, I keep Charlie in my lap, using him for the comfort I so badly seek.

The drink is set down next to me on the end table, and Colin takes a seat on the coffee table in front of me. "You know, before I moved here, I used to travel for work quite a bit. I have more airline miles than I could use myself. We could book you some flights, so you know exactly when you'll get to see them again."

I sniffle and finally meet his caring gaze. "I can't take time off work just because I can't manage to let go of my best friends."

"Why not? They're not just your friends. I saw that this weekend. Ella and Kenzie are your family."

There's no judgement in his tone or the way he looks at me, and that finally allows me to breathe a little easier. "They really are my family. I don't know how I thought I could do this on my own."

Colin reaches for my legs. "I'd like to think you're not alone here."

His words hit me in the feels. There's a new tightness in my chest that has nothing to do with missing my friends and everything to do with the conversation that's been long overdue.

"How, though? I can't just be friends with you now. Not after everything that's happened between us. Yet, we can't keep seeing each other. Selfishly, I'm not ready to let you go yet, but we both know this can't last, no matter how much we wish otherwise."

Saying that out loud lifts a weight off me I didn't realize I'd been carrying. Even if breaking up with Colin will hurt like hell, it's better to do it when it's on our own terms and not because we were forced to because of work.

His hold on my thighs tightens, and I finally release Sir Charles to accept Colin's comfort. The cat jumps onto the other couch cushion with a soft meow before circling and laying down within my reach.

Colin turns his palms upward, and I place my hands in his. He is biting his lip and avoids my gaze for several beats.

"What is it?" I ask, hoping the dread that's clawing its way up my throat isn't as real as it feels.

"Let me get some biscuits to go with tea before I tell you." He's up and out of the family room before I can ask what's going on with him.

Oh, God. Did Steve finally say something? I'd stupidly assumed that no news was good news, but maybe Colin had been shielding me from whatever happened since I've been out of the office. Have I already lost my job?

Breathing becomes harder, and I lean forward to put my head lower as I try to get my shit together. I grab on to the coffee table and attempt to think more positive thoughts, but it's really fucking hard in the moment with my emotions already all over the place.

Colin's laptop pings with a new email, and I can't stop my eyes from looking up at the screen that's right in front of me.

The subject of the email is "Piper's Chapters", and the

sender is Steve, but it's a reply to an earlier email. Colin doesn't have his email set up like mine. I can't see the body of the message. Only a short preview. One that makes bile rise in my throat.

Did Piper make her choice yet? I need to know...

I move to click on the email, but Colin walks back into the room. My heart is breaking even as I look up at him. "What did you do?"

"Fuck," he mutters before setting the plate of cookies on the table and reaching for me.

I jerk away from him. "Tell me what that email is talking about, Colin."

He takes a deep, shuddering breath as he sits next to me again. "Please, try to keep an open mind as I explain what happened and know that none of this was supposed to happen the way it did."

"What happened?" My words are clipped, and I'm not sure how to process the thoughts that are running through my mind as I wait for him to explain.

"The morning you sent those chapters to me, Steve came to me right after I'd read them. He said we needed to have a meeting and when we got to his office, he told me he saw us at the movies and that I had to end things with you. When I told him I couldn't do that, he said then we both might be fired."

"So you sent him my chapters to save your ass? Was that your plan all along? To throw me under the bus for writing?" I snarl. He's not painting a pretty picture so far.

His head shakes frantically. "No, and absolutely not. My plan was to—"

I can't take anymore. I stand up abruptly, scaring the hell out of the cat and cutting off Colin when I shout, "Enough. It doesn't matter what your plan was. You violated my privacy in the worst way. You knew I was nervous about those chapters. You know how hard it was to share that part of me with you. You had no right to share them with anyone else."

I'm halfway to the kitchen when he reaches for me. "Piper, please hear me out. It's not what you think, love. I wasn't trying to hurt you."

I laugh in his face, pulling further away from him. "Well, you sure did a bang-up job of that. Just leave me alone."

"Please, don't leave like this," he begs as I get to the door leading to the garage, but I don't bother to respond.

My heavy feet carry me forward, and I don't hear Colin follow when I close it loudly behind me.

I came to him so that he could make me feel better, but now, all I feel is regret.

Regret for moving here. For going to that club and kissing him. For allowing anything else to happen. For being all alone and having no one else to truly blame except myself.

Chapter Thirty

FUCK

Colin

ONCE THE SHOCK OF PIPER'S REACTION BEGINS TO wane, I rush after her, but when I get inside the garage, the automatic door is already opening and she's climbing into her car. Even still, I know I have to try to get her to hear me out.

"Piper, wait. I was only trying to help—"

She cuts me off with a glare and sharp tone. "Help who? Because if you really think what you did was for my benefit, then you're not who I thought."

I rush forward, hoping to reach her before she has the chance to back out. "It isn't like that. I swear. You might not realize it, but the way you talked about your book..." I let my sentence trail off when her head begins to shake.

"Colin, how I feel about anything else is irrelevant right now. You crossed a line. One I can't pretend doesn't hurt me deeply."

She gets in her car and shuts the door when I approach. I press my palm against the window and kneel so I can see

247

her face. She's looking forward, a tremble in her tight jaw. "Please, Piper. Don't leave like this."

When she doesn't move or reply, I allow myself the small hope that she'll hear the rest of what I wanted to say, but then she mutters, "Goodbye, Colin." And my chest feels like it's caving in.

I don't get another word out before she starts backing up and exiting the garage without giving me another look.

Damn it. This is so much worse than any of the scenarios I predicted. I'd thought she would at least hear me out. Sure, I did this partly so we could be together, but a big piece of me just wants to see Piper do something for herself that she's been hiding for so long.

She's a damn talented writer and the world should know that as well.

"Fuck," I snarl while I head back inside. I royally screwed things up, but I'm not giving up. Even if I have to write her a letter so she can know everything, I won't walk away from her without having tried everything I can think of to make things right.

If she still doesn't want me, then I'll quit Alliteration and let her live in peace. This is an all-or-nothing situation for me, and I'm willing to risk everything for her. No matter where I end up when things settle.

Chapter Thirty-One

A FAVOR

Piper

I sent an SOS text to Kenzie and Ella, but since they're still in the air, I spend several hours pacing, rage-cleaning, and blasting music through my house in an attempt to drown out my thoughts.

It's hard to believe that Colin shared my work with someone he had no right to. Work he knew I'd been overly private about. Work I thought he understood is incredibly special to me.

Clearly, I'd been wrong to believe he was as perfect as he'd seemed.

The worst part is that the longer I stew on what happened, the more I realize that I'm done here. There's no way I can continue working for him, and I don't see the point in staying in LA if I can't do the work I love.

No, I'll be going home with my tail between my legs, and I'll even owe Alliteration money for my moving expenses since I signed a one-year employment contract.

Damn it. Why did Colin have to do this?

Maybe it's better this happened. There was no way for our relationship to work out. A messy ending was bound to happen. I just didn't expect that to be at my expense.

Finally, my phone rings and it's a video chat from Kenzie's phone, but she and Ella are both on the screen when I answer.

"What the hell happened?" Ella asks with a frown, and I see a restaurant booth behind them.

I rub a hand over my face and let out a heavy sigh as I lean back against my headboard. "I don't even know. I was so upset after leaving the airport and Colin was trying to make me feel better by saying all these nice things, but then he admitted to doing something he thought would help for some asinine reason. Instead, all he did was break my trust in the worst way possible."

Kenzie snarls. "Did the fucker cheat?"

"Okay, maybe not the worst way, but still awful. He gave the chapters of my book to his boss Steve." My sadness has begun to wane and is replaced by anger. So much anger from the betrayal I feel.

Kenzie and Ella share a look, and I'm confused why they're not raging on my behalf. Confused and frustrated, because I need their support right now.

"Um, Pipe. Did you consider that maybe he did you a favor?" Kenzie asks, her tone soft and curious.

My eyes bulge, and my chest tightens. "Excuse me? Why would I think that?"

The two of them share another too-long-for-my-liking gaze. Any calm I'd been trying to hold on to snaps. "What aren't you guys saying?" I demand.

Ella sighs, a small smile lifting on her face as she takes the phone so that I can see only her. "Piper, you know we love you unconditionally, and we're so proud of all you've accomplished with this job, but you've been miserable ever since you started editing full-time. I don't think you've noticed it, but coming to visit you, we see things clearer now."

"See what?" I ask, my voice barely above a whisper.

Ella continues, "The only time you glowed about your work while we were there was when you talked about the book. We thought before you left that you'd only been *meh* about editing because you weren't settled, but now that you are, you still don't seem to have the love for it like you think you do. At least, that's how it feels from the outside looking in."

My head shakes in disbelief. I don't understand what they're saying, and I really need them to help make me feel better. Yet, they're only confusing me more. I love helping my authors make their books shine.

Kenzie steals the phone back and grins. "Don't look at us like that. We're only saying these things because we love you and would have said them before, but none of it really came together until Ella started reading the pages you sent her."

"What do you mean? What does my book have to do with any of this other than Colin sending those chapters to someone he had no right or reason to?" I feel dead inside. I can't remember a day when I've felt worse or more alone.

Kenzie sighs, but her tone remains kind. "The book has everything to do with this. Did Colin tell you why he shared those chapters?"

I shrug, then wipe away the new tears on my cheeks. "I didn't really give him the chance to. He said Steve threatened to fire us if we didn't break up, so he shared them likely to save his own ass."

Ella frowns. "That doesn't seem like something the

man you've talked about these past two months and who we got to know over the last five days would do."

No, it doesn't, but there's no other reason I can think of as to why Colin would have done what he did.

"How did you find out that the chapters were shared?" Kenzie asks.

"He was working on the couch when I got there. His laptop was open, and an email came through from Steve. I could only see a small part of it, but he was asking if I'd made my decision. Probably wondering if I'd decided to quit, which sounds like a really fucking great idea right now."

Kenzie and Ella share another look, and if they were in front of me, I'd be trying to choke them both. "What the hell aren't the two of you saying?"

Ella brushes her hair back and smiles at me through the camera. "As Kenzie said before, I started reading the chapters you emailed me when we were on the plane. I may not read as much as you do, but I've read enough to know the story you've created is damn good. Good enough to publish. Have you considered that Colin wasn't trying to get you fired, but that he sees what we do and is giving you the opportunity you might not have ever given yourself?"

My chest feels hollow. Breathing is painful, and my throat burns with emotion while my trembling hands are doing a shit job of holding up the phone.

A publishing deal? Could Colin have asked Steve to consider making me an offer? I don't have an agent or any real experience. I'm not even close to ready for the submission process that normally takes years for most authors.

No, this couldn't be what that email is about.

Right?

The fact that I'm no longer sure makes me want to vomit, and I have no clue what I'm supposed to do with these thoughts now.

"Take a deep breath, Pipe," Kenzie says. "We're right here, and everything is going to be okay. I know Colin should have asked for your permission, but if Steve was threatening to fire both of you, then maybe there was no other choice."

I want to argue that there is always another choice, but I can't. A weariness settles over me, and I decide I can't do this anymore. I need time to process and think on my own.

"I love you both, but I need to go, and my phone might be off for a while. I need time to think and process what happened today," I say wearily.

Kenzie tilts her head and speaks softly. "You know if you talked to Colin, you'd have more answers."

I nod. "I won't ignore him forever. I just need a day or two."

Ella blows me a kiss. "Take whatever time you need, and remember we're here for you whenever you need us."

"Thank you," I whisper before ending the video chat and dropping my phone on the couch.

What the hell am I going to do now?

Chapter Thirty-Two

THE LAST TIME

Colin

PIPER'S PHONE HAS BEEN OFF EVERY TIME I'VE called her, and she hasn't responded to the few texts I've sent. I'm trying not to be pushy, but not knowing if she's okay is killing me. It was never my intention to hurt her. I only wanted to make things better, yet they're now worse than they ever were before.

My phone rings, and I see Steve's name on the screen. Shit. I'm not ready to talk to him, but if I don't take the call, I won't know what he's going to do.

"Good morning, Steve," I answer, but even I can hear the flatness in my voice.

"Morning, indeed. You haven't responded to my email. Am I to assume that Piper isn't interested in my proposal?" he asks.

It's time to come clean.

"Piper doesn't know about your proposal yet. She's not exactly speaking to me at the moment, but when I talk to her, I will make sure she knows."

His sigh of disappointment is clear, even through the phone. "I had a feeling that might be the case. Do you understand why we no longer allow relationships within the departments? You've made quite the situation for yourself, Colin. What do you expect me to do?"

He isn't wrong. If I was him, I know what I would do, but I'm hoping he's a better boss than I would be.

"I'd expect you to fire me for causing trouble within the workplace, but I'd like to ask for more time. At least enough so that Piper knows what really happened. I don't want her hurt to pay for my poor decisions."

Steve is silent for several beats. "Until the end of today, Colin. That's all I can offer you. Find a way to salvage this before it gets out of hand for the both of us."

A sharp pain shoots through my chest and I close my eyes for a brief moment. I'm not sure there is anything left to "salvage," but I badly want to hope there is. "Thank you, Steve."

"You'll be in the office soon?" he asks.

"Yeah. I just need to do something and then I'll be there," I say, already knowing I have to figure out a way to get in touch with Piper and explain myself.

After we hang up, I take a second to consider my options. She won't answer my calls or texts, so my only other option is to show up at her house. Though, if she doesn't open the door, that doesn't help things, either.

I decide it's time to put pen to paper and write her a letter. That way I can at least leave it in her mailbox. If she still doesn't respond in some way, then I'll solve our problems for her. I'll quit Alliteration and no longer be the reason she feels like she can't go to work.

It's not something I want to do, but I refuse to hurt Piper any more than I already have. As soon as I find paper,

I get to scribbling the words I wanted to tell her last night and ones I hope I get to tell her in person, but this will be better than nothing.

Piper,

First, I want to apologize for violating your trust. I crossed a line I shouldn't have. No matter my reason, I should have put you first and I didn't. I'm sorry.

Steve approached me last week about seeing us at the movies. It was the morning you emailed me those chapters. If he'd given me more time, I had a plan that included having your permission for what I did, but there was no time. I was faced with the choice of losing you, getting us fired, or doing something radical.

I asked Steve to consider offering you a publishing deal instead of the former options. I know you don't think you're ready for this, but I believe in you, Piper. I see the spark in your eyes when you talk about your book, and I hear the passion in your voice.

Very few people in this world get to do the thing that makes them happy, and I want that for you even if I'm not part of it. You have real talent the world won't want to miss out on.

I'm sorry this is how it happened, but Steve does want to make an offer on your book if you're interested. (I hope you are.) One that would allow you to move back to North Carolina and be with your family again. Another thing I know would make you happy.

If you won't talk to me, please at least speak with Steve and consider your options before you turn them down. You deserve this, Piper. I just wish I hadn't screwed things up so badly so you could enjoy this moment the way you should.

I hope to hear from you soon, but if I don't, then I'll take that to mean you're done with me. I don't want to be the reason you don't feel comfortable coming to Alliteration in whatever manner that is moving forward. If we're done, then I can promise I won't ever interfere with your life again.

I really am sorry, and even though I don't deserve it, I hope somehow I can earn your forgiveness.

I wish you only happiness, little bird.

With love,

Colin

Signing off on that letter has my hand shaking and heart racing out of my chest. Leaving LA and never seeing Piper again terrifies me, but it's the only way I can think of to make this somewhat right if she refuses to speak with me.

With that done, I grab an envelope and put the folded letter inside, then I give Charlie a long head-rub. "Wish me luck, furball."

He meows, making me smile for the first time since Piper walked out.

I don't want to wait any longer, so I grab my keys and head out the door. It only takes two minutes to get to Piper's and I don't see her car, but that doesn't mean anything. She parks in the garage half the time anyway.

Parking and walking up to her door are painful. Fear like I've never known before nearly swallows me and makes my feet feel like they each weigh a ton.

When I get to her door, I take a shuddering inhale before forcing the air back up. My grip on the envelope is tight, and I really hope I don't have to leave this for her.

My finger presses on the doorbell button, and I listen to the chimes sound inside the house. I move my head closer to the door, but there is nothing else that I can hear. No music or TV or footfalls.

I wait a couple minutes, then try knocking instead. Still,

the seconds tick by and the heaviness over my chest is suffocating.

There's a mailbox hanging next to her door, so I drop the letter into that and listen one last time, but still nothing other than silence greets my ears.

With dread drowning me, I head back to my car and drive to work. Possibly for the last time.

Chapter Thirty-Three

KEEP YOU

Piper

THE SKY IS GROWING DARK OUTSIDE WHEN I WAKE up. Wait, no. The sun isn't setting, it's just now starting to rise. With a groan, I try to sit up but have to lay back down, thanks to the pounding in my head.

"Holy hell, what did I do?" I mutter, slowly rolling to the edge of my bed.

My feet dangle off the side, and I rub at my temples before glancing at my clock that flashes 5:13am.

Shit. I slept for over thirteen hours. I guess emotional exhaustion will do that to a person. And possibly staying up for more than twenty-four hours.

After I got off the phone with Ella and Kenzie, I had a strong desire to write. To see the words of my nearly finished story come together. To see for myself if my friends and Colin might have been right.

To see that I'd just been too damn scared to take a chance on myself and see what happens.

I don't even know how many words I typed throughout

the previous night and day, but it was as if my fingers had been possessed, and there was nothing I could do to stop them once the words started pouring out of me.

I didn't expect that to happen, but I'm glad it did because they'd all been right. Creating this world? Writing this story? There isn't a joy in my life that I can compare to it. Sure, I have immensely enjoyed helping other authors over the years since I entered the publishing world, but I can clearly see now that what I thought was happiness before was only contentment.

I hop into the shower and go through my morning routine with new intentions on my mind today. I need to see Colin. It's been over a day and a half since I talked to him, and I need to apologize for not hearing him out and accept his apology for sharing my chapters. Well, as long as he swears it won't ever happen again.

He might not have gone about doing things the right way, but based on what I've been putting together since talking to Ella and Kenzie, I no longer believe he was trying to hurt me or acting selfishly. Well, maybe a little, but still. I think there is still something between us that is worth fighting for.

Once I'm done getting ready, it's just after six in the morning. Deciding I can't wait any longer, I take the chance that Colin is awake and get in my car.

When I get there, I spot Sir Charles in the window and grin. That cat is too adorable for his own good.

My hands are shaking as I open my door and step out of the car. I walk hesitantly up to the porch, then pat my pockets and curse. I forgot my phone. I maybe should have called first, but it's too late now.

I knock on the door and wait silently for him to answer. I hear Charlie's meow and don't see him in the window anymore. I assume he's gone to let Colin know I'm there, but then I hear him again and this time much closer.

A couple minutes tick by and this time I ring the doorbell. Maybe he's in the shower. I pace in front of his door and decide it's pointless after knocking a second time. The only noise I can hear is the meowing of Charlie who can't open the door for me.

I get back in my car and head home to grab my bag and phone for work. After running upstairs, I grumble. "Of course, it's dead. Why wouldn't it be when I need to make a call?"

Deciding to use my car charger, I go back to my vehicle and toss my stuff onto the passenger's seat before plugging my phone in.

I'm on the road within seconds and headed toward Alliteration. If Colin isn't home, then maybe he's there. I'll do a drive-through of the parking garage, and if I don't see his car, then hopefully I'll be able to get a hold of him by phone.

There's hardly any traffic on the side streets this early, and I make it to work in record time. When I get to the first level of the parking garage, I don't see Colin's Lexus in the area where it normally is, but that doesn't stop me from continuing on.

By the time I get to the third level of parking, I haven't spotted him and grow frustrated, then remember my phone.

The stupid thing is still off. "Damn it." The charging cord isn't all the way pushed into the USB port.

"You've got to be kidding me." Slamming my fist on the steering wheel, I fix the issue and make my way down to where we normally park, so I can wait for my phone to turn on and keep an eye out for Colin.

While I'm sitting in the car, constantly pressing the power button on my phone as if that will make it turn on faster, there's a knock on my window.

A yelp echoes inside my car as I look up to find Steve staring down at me. He waves, and I roll down my window.

"What are you doing, Piper?" he asks casually.

I glance around and don't see anyone else. "I was, uh, charging my phone." I hold it up and give the device a good shaking for emphasis.

"I see. So, you're not hiding out here, hoping to avoid a certain boss of yours?" His graying brow raises, and I remember that Steve knows our secret.

My shoulders fall. "I'm sorry."

He leans closer, resting his forearms on my door. "As you should be. The two of you broke your contracts, but what I'm even more sad about is losing Colin as an employee when I hoped that his solution was going to work for all of us."

"Excuse me?" I feel like my eyes are going to fall out of their sockets at any moment, and the agony I'd been feeling yesterday is back with a vengeance. "Did you fire him?"

Steve frowns and shakes his head. "You two are terrible at communicating. No, I didn't. He quit yesterday before he left for the day. He was already here this morning packing up his office. He didn't want to cause you any further discomfort, but maybe he was wrong to assume that's the way you feel."

Damn Colin for being so considerate. Damn him for making me feel so much.

My head rests back against my seat, and I let out a shuddering breath. I don't know how to fix this now. Everything has gone wrong so quickly.

Steve clears his throat, and I open my eyes to find him

still staring at me. "I know this isn't my place, but if I may be frank…" I nod, and he continues, "Colin showed me your work, and I promised him I wouldn't say anything until you came to me, but I think maybe I should. You have real talent, Piper. I realize now that your editing skills are above par because you have real passion inside you for creating. That's not something an author can learn."

I can feel the flush covering my cheeks as he speaks. "Thank you."

"You're welcome, but if you really want to thank me, come see me and bring me more chapters, so I can make you a proper offer. One that will benefit both you and this company for years to come, if you want it to."

My pulse is racing, but this time it's not because I'm afraid, but because I'm truly thrilled to hear Steve say that. I know I'd assumed it before, but hearing the words out loud for the first time…is something else entirely.

"I will do that. Just as soon as I find Colin."

Steve's hand pats the frame of my door. "Do that, and convince him to rescind his resignation. It's not too late to undo all of this."

Oh, how I hope he's right.

As soon as Steve moves away from my car, I check my phone once more. There are several texts from Colin, Ella, and Kenzie, but I don't bother to read any of them.

Me: I'll be at your house soon. Please be there.

I press send and hope Colin sees my message and is already headed home.

As quickly, yet safely, as I can manage, I work my way through the growing morning traffic. Twenty painful minutes later, I finally pull up to Colin's.

His garage is open with his car parked half outside. The doors are open, and I can see boxes stacked inside the vehicle. I assume they're from his office, but maybe he's already getting things ready to move...

Is it possible he's leaving LA so soon?

God, I hope not.

Colin comes staggering out of his garage with two more boxes. He can't see me around the cardboard, and I scare the hell out of him when I say, "Hi."

He drops the top box, which lands on his foot, causing the other box to go crashing toward the ground. A painful groan sounds from his lips, and I step forward to help, but he's bouncing around so much, I'm not sure what to do.

"Bloody hell, that hurt," he mutters before finally settling still. His eyes have dark circles under them, and it doesn't seem as if he's shaved in the last forty-ish hours since I've seen him. "I'm sorry."

I tilt my head and frown. "Sorry for me scaring you and causing you to drop those boxes?"

He steps forward, then pauses. "Sorry for everything. I don't know if you got my letter, but before I leave, I just need you to know I never wanted to hurt you, Piper. Doing so will be the greatest regret of my life."

His voice is thick with emotion, and all I want to do is soothe his worries. I walk closer to him, sidestepping one of the boxes, and reach for his hands. He squeezes back and sucks in a harsh breath.

"I'm sorry, too," I say. "I should have listened to you, but I was scared and angry. I didn't see a letter from you. Though, now I want to go home and find it, but that can wait. What I mean to say is I understand better now. I spent hours writing and I was able to see things differently. When I was done, I passed out and my phone died... I wasn't trying to ignore you for so long."

He grins widely and gathers me into his arms. "You

have no reason to apologize. We wouldn't be in this situation if I had handled things better."

I step back and shake my head. "You're right. We probably would have been in a worse situation, because I don't think I could have ever been ready to accept that maybe writing is what I'd rather be doing until I hit the low I had. I needed the push to see things clearly. Now, we just need you to get your job back. He told me you quit, which is absolutely ridiculous by the way."

Colin kisses my forehead. "Nothing is ridiculous when you're hurting. When you didn't come into work and didn't respond to any of my attempts at contact, I didn't know what else to do. You deserve better than the hurt I caused. Even if you forgive me, I'm still not there yet. I deserve to lose my job."

I sigh. "Not happening. You'd get sent back to London, and that doesn't work for me. Steve said you can still rescind the resignation, and if you want my true forgiveness, you better do that."

His fingers stroke my cheeks, and there is a spark back in his gray eyes that I've missed these last two days. "What if I don't go back to work for Steve?"

I'm not sure how to respond to that, because I don't know what else he would do besides go back to London, which wouldn't give us the ending I'm hoping for.

"What if I tell Steve that I'll still work for Alliteration, but I want whatever job I can get in North Carolina?"

My mouth opens and closes, but no words come out. In all of my thinking, I hadn't considered moving back home as an option. I mean, I should have. Working with Alliteration on a publishing deal doesn't mean I need to be in LA.

"Seriously? You'd leave here for me?" I finally croak out.

He nods, rubbing his thumb over the top of my hand. "After seeing how close the three of you are and how much you were hurting after your friends left, I knew keeping you from them was never going to make you happy in the long run."

I throw my arms around his neck and kiss his lips, then around his whole face as I pull him closer to me. "Thank you. Thank you so damn much."

His forehead presses against mine, and he smiles softly. "I love you, Piper. There isn't anything I wouldn't do to make you happy."

My heart leaps from my chest to my throat, and I roughly press my lips to his again. "I love you, too. So much it hurts."

His tongue sweeps inside my mouth, and he bends me backward, kissing me so thoroughly that I can hardly breathe when he lifts me back up.

"Get these boxes out of your car. You're not moving. Yet," I say, needing him naked and in his bed as soon as possible.

"These were book donations I was going to make to the library, but if I don't have to ship them overseas again, then I will gladly keep them."

I grip his shirt tightly. "And I will gladly keep you."

Epilogue

NOW AND FOREVER

Colin

Eighteen Months Later

It's been a wild ride ever since Piper forgave me. A ride I never could have predicted, but one I've enjoyed the hell out of.

As I stand at the barbeque in our backyard and watch our friends laugh while playing cornhole, I can't think of anywhere else I'd rather be.

Piper walks toward me, smiling from ear to ear and eating one of Celia's famous dick cookies. Bentley tried to get me to veto them at our house, but that wasn't happening according to Piper. Celia hadn't been someone I heard too much about until after talks of moving to North Carolina started. Bentley's sister is now an integral part of their girl gang, and I learned early on not to question the things those women do. The four of them together can instill very real fear in a man.

"How's my superstar wife?" I ask teasingly while wiping a bit of crumbs from the corner of her mouth with my thumb. She's practically glowing, and she should be, considering all that's been happening.

She shoves me lightly. "Unsure why you're calling her a superstar, but joyous nonetheless."

I tap my chin dramatically. "Hmm, I wonder. Maybe it's because her debut book has been on the *New York Times* and *USA Today* bestseller lists for four weeks in a row, and she has movie producers sniffing around?"

The blush that covers her cheeks only makes me love her more. She published that wolf shifter book just last month under a pseudonym that she, Kenzie, and Ella came up with: Aria Collins. I'd voted for her to at least use Piper, but she insisted on some sort of anonymity just in case things went south. Plus, I couldn't complain much when she used my first name in the surname.

Now, I'm thinking the pseudonym is going to be better to give her a semblance of privacy.

She leans up on her toes and kisses me. "In case I haven't told you lately... Thank you for believing in me, even when I wanted to give up so many times, and for giving me all of this."

She turns around and gestures to Ella, Owen, Kenzie, Bentley, Celia, and her fiancé Aiden standing across the yard. Tears build in her eyes.

"No thanks needed. I'm pretty sure I got more out of this deal than you did," I say with a wink.

We moved to North Carolina just six months after Piper signed her book deal. Just as I hoped, the changes within the company that were already in the works opened up a spot at the publishing house here that Piper used to work for and, even though it was a pay cut, I took the editor position without question.

Telling Piper that we were moving to North Carolina was the second greatest day of my life. The first being when she became my wife the month after we got here.

Behind us, Ella runs toward the house with a worried Owen right behind her. Piper's eyes go wide, and she turns to look at Kenzie, who is already shrugging.

My hand rubs Piper's back. "I'm sure she's fine."

She nods, but her eyes don't stray from the back door. Ella and Owen have been struggling with fertility issues, which has undoubtedly caused strain between the two of them, but we all keep hoping and praying that they'll get the baby they so badly desire.

A bark and playful growl distract us momentarily from the concern. I glance over to find Kenzie and Bentley's dog running from Bentley with two bean bags from the game in his mouth.

"Zeus, drop it," he demands, and I swear I see laughter in the dog's eyes. "I mean it, dog. Give those back."

The massive beast just waggles his tail and runs right around Bentley, who then turns to point at his wife. "This is your fault. You picked the most devious dog on purpose."

Kenzie blows him a kiss. "I thought you loved *devious* since you married me."

He grumbles something I can't hear, and I chuckle, wrapping an arm around Piper. "We should get one of those."

"A dog? Really?" she asks.

I shrug. "That. Or we can try for a baby and see what happens."

She blinks rapidly, then finally grins. "Too bad we can't start trying right now."

My hands tug her flush against me. "Who says we can't? Wouldn't be the first time we've snuck off," I whisper against her lips.

She kisses me softly. "As much as I want to say yes, I need to go check on Ella."

Kenzie and Celia are already headed our way and Kenzie snags Piper's arm before I can give my wife another kiss.

"Come on. Let's go put our noses where we know they belong," the redhead says with an evil glint in her eyes.

Though, before they can make it far, Owen and Ella come through the door, both with grins on their faces.

Piper covers her mouth and squeals, while Kenzie lets out an excited, "Fuck, yeah!" and Celia starts to tear up, waving a hand in front of her eyes.

Confusion fills me until Ella nods and starts crying and laughing at the same time. Owen backs away, and all four women hug in a tangle of arms and flying hair as they jump together.

Bentley and Aiden join me. "What's happening?" the former asks.

"No damn clue, mate," I say.

Owen grasps my and Bentley's shoulders but looks at all three of us. "How do each of you feel about becoming uncles?"

"No shit?" Bentley says, then glances behind Owen. "You're sure?"

Owen nods with a huge grin plastered to his face. "Yep. The doctor called with confirmation while she was throwing up just now. She's ten weeks along and has been sick daily. Apparently, that's a great sign. Though, it feels weird to celebrate my wife vomiting."

Aiden nods and gives a slight shudder. "I remember

hearing my mom get sick when I was a teen and then being really confused when she'd celebrate. In her defense, she'd lost a few babies before my baby sister and never told me. I'd had no clue until I was an adult. Just roll with it, man."

Owen's grin stretches across his face. "Oh, I plan to do more than roll with it."

My chest swells and I'm beyond happy for them after everything Piper had shared with me about their attempts to conceive, but I'm even more excited for my wife to be ready for the same thing. Apparently, I'm the only one standing here thinking that way.

Bentley groans. "Don't take this the wrong way, O...but now they're all going to want babies and I can barely control the damn dog. What the fuck am I supposed to do with a child?"

Owen and I both laugh at him and Aiden, who is now cringing, and suddenly everything feels right.

———

Piper

"Please, don't break my hand," I beg Ella as my fingers start to go numb.

She snarls at me. "Tell your niece to quit trying to break my vagina!"

Owen winces and strokes her hair back. "Amelia isn't trying to break anything. She's just eager to meet you. Don't you want to see whose eyes and nose she has?"

Ella takes several deep breaths before nodding. "I guess."

The doctor's head pops back up. "Last push if you can give it your best."

The glare Ella cuts toward her doctor frightens even me. "I'll show you my best."

Owen and I share a look of dread, then I glance at the opening door.

Kenzie comes in with coffee and balloons, then nearly drops both. "Shit. I almost missed the action."

I gladly let Kenzie step in, taking Ella's death grip from my withered hand. Lucky Celia is still an hour out thanks to a supply run she had to do today and is missing the physical abuse I've been enduring.

Ella's grunts and screams are so loud that I'm sure the rest of the hospital can hear her, and it makes me worry about what I'll be like in just six months.

"That's it, Ella. Give me everything you have left. I just need one more solid push," the doc says with her face buried between Ella's legs.

"It burns," my best friend screams.

Kenzie makes the mistake of snickering. "I read that's called the ring of fire." Not even a second later, Kenzie is nearly on her knees. "Damn it, woman. Ease up."

I lean closer to Kenzie. "I wouldn't mention any more rings of fire for at least several weeks."

She scoffs. "Now you tell me."

Ella screams one last time while Owen and I bring her knees up, helping her to push harder.

"I hate you all so fucking much right now," she says just before her body goes limp.

The doctor chuckles, and a shuddering cry captures our attention. "Don't hate me too much. I want to introduce you to your son."

My hand covers my face while Owen and Ella gasp, then Kenzie laughs. "You've got to be shitting us?"

Doc pulls the blanket back after settling the tiny little human on Ella's chest. "Nope. No shitting around here, thankfully."

As she goes back to tending to whatever is going down below for Ella, all of us just shrug and laugh. What else can we do?

Ella strokes his little scruff of hair. "I guess you're going to need a new name, little one."

"And a new room," Owen mutters, but the awe on his face is undeniable.

Kenzie and I lean forward together, get our peeks, then give Ella a squeeze. "You three get to know each other and we'll be back soon," I say.

"Thank you," Ella says to us before we leave to find our husbands.

———

LATER THAT NIGHT, COLIN AND I ARE HOME FROM the hospital and lying in bed. I should be exhausted, but the adrenaline from watching my not-niece be born has yet to ease.

"I can't believe Amelia is actually an Asher," Colin says, kissing my belly. "Maybe we shouldn't find out. Might be safer that way."

My hands grip the sides of his head, and I narrow my eyes at his perfect face. "Not a chance in hell."

His chuckle over my stomach sends shivers up my spine and I involuntarily push closer to him. "How are my chances looking at making love to my wife when she's been awake for more than twenty-four hours?"

"Pretty damn good," I say, reaching for his shoulders.

A thud sounds at the end of the bed, followed by a meow, and I see Sir Charles saunter his way toward us. He's been extra needy since I found out I was pregnant.

"And there go my chances," Colin deadpans when I reach for the cat.

I scratch his back and give him a kiss on the nose. "Give Mommy and Daddy some time alone and I'll give you the special treats."

I swear the cat is too smart. He presses his head against mine, purrs loudly, then runs from the room.

Colin grins, then kisses my tiny baby bump once more before climbing further over me. "I love you so fucking much some days that I think my chest is going to explode."

"I feel like I should be sorry about that, but I'm really not," I tease, then capture his mouth with mine.

Our tongues tangle while Colin's hands move slowly up my sides, tugging my nightgown up as he goes.

Once the soft fabric is out of our way, I reach for his boxer briefs to find they're already gone. "Cocky much?"

He bites at my neck. "Just hopeful you'd choose me over the furball." His hand lifts my thigh until my ankle is level with his head. "I really want to tie you to this bed and have my way with you, but I don't think I can wait, either."

"Then, don't," I beg.

As much as I love his wild ways in the bedroom, some nights I just need my husband and nothing else. After an emotional day, this is one of those nights.

The head of his cock rubs against my clit, causing me to flinch with need.

"Your wish is my command." Colin enters me in one swift motion, and I still dig my nails into his arms, even all these months later.

Our gazes lock, and the amount of love from him that I feel penetrating into my soul nearly takes my breath away.

He rocks against me and runs his fingers over my chest in a circular motion. "I love you, little bird."

"I love you, too, my handsome husband."

My hands reach for his face and tug him closer as his hips start to move again in slow, deep thrusts.

The pace of our kiss matches the pace of our lovemaking, and I can't help from smiling against his soft lips.

Never in my life did I expect to meet this wonderful man or have things turn out the way they did, but not for one second do I regret any choice or the bumps in the road that got us to this moment.

Together. Now and forever. Because nothing has ever felt more right than being with Colin and carrying our child.

Thank you so much for reading the final book in my Unexpected Series!
If you want to chat about all things RomComs and get all the latest updates about what's coming next, join my RomCom Insiders group and keep flipping the pages for more info!

Connect with Me

Want to come hang out with me on social media and with other readers who also enjoyed books this one? Join Harper Reed's RomCom Insiders for fun and shenanigans!
Also, check out the many ways to connect with me below! These are the best ways to stay updated on new releases and sales.

Newsletter—Reader Group—Facebook Page—Instagram—TikTok—Website—Amazon—Bookbub

I look forward to seeing you around!

Also by Harper Reed

Acknowledgments

When I first started on this journey back in 2019, I failed. Epicly. I never even managed to write one word in the story I wanted. Then, nearly two years later, my desire to write RomComs was just as strong as ever.

I still wasn't sure I could do this and do it the way I wanted, but with a small team behind me, I finally did! I took the chance and I'm so thankful to the readers who embraced this unknown author and her crazy stories!

I'm also thankful for my assistant Kelly Stepp who handled all of those little details for me that I would have never thought of. You are amazing and I shall keep you in my pocket forever!

My editor and best friend who has, until now, remained unnamed... Jamie Holmes. I love you, my asstie, bestie boo. Thank you for not quitting on me even when I know there were days you were tempted. Oops!

To my other assistant Michelle Fitz who helped me keep this secret while still being my emotional support person. All the love!

To Jane Catherine... you are always a positive and supportive bright light in my life. Thank you for being *you*!!

To the lovely UK readers who read the first draft of this story and helped me make Colin a little more true to his roots! Biff Wharton, Jo McQuaid, and Colleen Van Dyk. I appreciate all three of you!

To my other readers, who I've kept this secret from, thank you for not throwing stones while I put my other writing on hold to do something that made me oh-so happy! Have you figured me out already?

If not, flip one more page!

About the Author

Harper Reed is a Romantic Comedy author. She lives in the beautiful state of Oregon with her husband of twenty years. While Harper is new to the genre, she has been reading RomCom's for decades and has published several dozen books in varying genres over the years.
You can find her other works under Heather Renee.
In her downtime, Harper enjoys reading, going on escapades with her husband, and spending time outdoors. She looks forward to this new branch of her author career and can't wait to bring you more deliciously comical books!
Want to learn more? Visit her website www. HarperReedBooks.com to see upcoming books and ways to connect with her.